Published by:

The Power of Words – SA

Contact Details:

Website Author https://nadinemay.company.site/

Author's blog : the End of Time: https://nadinemay.com/

Novel Blog : https://allrealityshifters.wordpress.com/

The Language of Light workbooks and journals: https://lightworkerjournals.wordpress.com

ISBN: ebook 978-1-0672285-1-4

ISBN: print 978-1-0672285-0-7

Previously published by Kima Global Publishers.

© Nadine May 2020

https://nadinemay.company.site/

Table of Contents

The *Self*-Employed Housewife

Diary of a foreigner.

A dream
Not
Interpreted
Is a
Letter
Not
Read

The *Self*-Employed Housewife

Volume Two

Nadine May

Acknowledgements

This sequel novel was inspired by my readers who wanted to follow the life of a self-Employed housewife

All the characters in this novel are fictitious to protect the people who shaped my life at often difficult times.

Foremost I must thank my publisher Robin Beck who has inspired me to write about Hendrika's thirty-three-year marriage and what it took to separate in Grace.

I must thank my children, their father and the many friends who were my support base during troubled times.

Being a self-employed housewife during times of many changes in South Africa forced me to awaken to the illusions of the realities we create. I learned to love being dyslexic and overcome a lack of self-esteem to become a published author.

Nadine May

Introduction

Her exposure to an inexplicable experience early one morning shatters her perception of life. How was she ever going to share it with anybody?

Her children were growing up, moving from primary school to high school followed by college, at a time when being a self-employed housewife was often challenged.

How would Hendrika ever learn to cope with feelings of loneliness, living in an empty marriage relationship, when she knew there was far more to life.

She asked for guidance and was shown a change of direction through dreams and visions.

Through her inner unhappiness, she learned that she had the power to change her life.

Her creativity in being an independent entrepreneur forced her to overcome her greatest obstacles. Only then would she find her Soul Purpose in life.

Chapter One

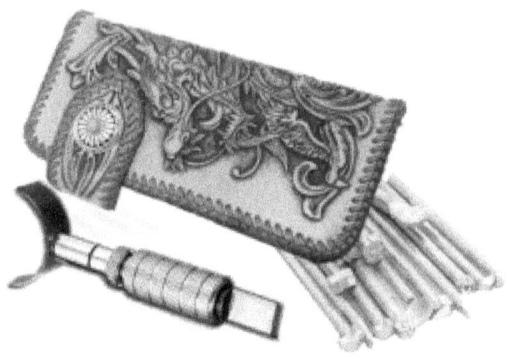

Visions from the Future?

"**M**ommy, are you okay?" Hendrika heard.

"Mommy, why are you sleeping in the lounge?" the little girl's quavering voice whispered close to her ear. The gooseflesh all over her whole body felt like she had been far away, but the ringing in her ears told her otherwise.

"Sonja, why are you home from school?"

"School is finished. I walked home."

With some difficulty, she sat up, leaning against the couch's backrest. Her surprise at seeing her children staring at her with big eyes made her smile. She would have got up if she had not felt nauseous and her aching body, as if a steamroller had flattened her. Her head was spinning.

"Mommy fell asleep. What time is it?"

"Lunchtime," Lucas said

"When did you get home, Lucas?" Her six-year-old class finished at twelve, while Sonja finished at two o'clock because she was two years older.

"Lucas was playing outside with the dog from next door when I came home." I first rang the bell, but the front door was not locked." Sonja replied, sounding all grown up. Gosh, why did she have a feeling that she had been away? Away from her life, away from who she was?

"Mommy, are you sick?"

That must be it. All of a sudden, she felt freezing, but the ringing had stopped, and so did her nausea.

"I feel...cold. Come, let's have something to eat." When she stood up from the couch, her feet felt numb and tingling, but after a few steps, the numbness was gone. She would have gone to bed if it were not for her children, but somehow, she knew she needed to eat. In the kitchen, the clock on the stove told her that she had slept for at least six hours! Had she been dreaming?

"Mommy, can we have a dog?" Lucas asked all of a sudden. Sonja wanted a cat and a bird. Not a very good combination.

"Oh, I'm not sure. Ask Daddy when he gets home."

She knew he was not keen to have a dog again like they had in Australia. The sadness at having to leave their cat and dog at the kennels when they had emigrated back to Holland three years ago was still too vivid, but one day, they would take a trip to the SPCA

"Is Daddy home for dinner?"

"No idea, Moppie." Vaguely, she recalled that he had left early that morning, before regular office hours, so there must have been an ore ship in. Jan was only handling them, and they did not come in daily.

Had she been Hallucinating?

After lunch, she was still rooted at the kitchen table in a daze while the kids had gone to their room to get changed out of their school uniforms. What had happened to her early this morning? Cigarettes! Someone told her to stop smoking, but whom? After dropping the kids off at school, she vividly recalled having her first cigarette.

She went outside to have a look at the outside barbeque. Yes, there it was. All the cigarettes she had cut up were still lying there.

The kids were arguing inside about who had the most prominent space on their dining room table to do their homework. Everything looked normal, but she felt far from it. The voice had been so clear as if someone had been in the room with her. If only she could tell somebody, but who would believe her?

"Hey, you two, Lucas, move to the other side of the table."

"But Sonja has more space, and that's not fair."

She had to snap out of her confusion. All she could do now was ask Pat at the second-hand bookshop if she had books about people who could hear voices from those who were not in the body. Gosh, that sounded so silly. Had she been hallucinating?

Being Dyslexic

"Come, Lucas, show me what homework you have. Let's do it together."

Her little boy was not like Sonja, who loved schoolwork. He was more like her but not as dyslexic as she had been at his age. His writing was not like Sonja's. He made more mistakes but was not dyslexic, which was a relief. She never got over her inability to write without making huge mistakes. She just never spotted them. While sailing with him on the ship, her dad had tried to teach her. He made her write down each letter in the alphabet. To her, they were just shapes and scribbles. Numbers were somehow more manageable, but she sometimes wrote them upside down or reversed them as she did with the p and the d. Her parents could never understand why she could not see this for herself.

Somehow, she didn't do that anymore, but there was no way she could ever write a note to the teacher. She would be far too embarrassed to be seen as being stupid.

"Mummy, can you check my reading?" Sonja asked. Lucas was happily clearing away his homework. Unlike Sonja, who was popular and had many friends, he didn't like school and was a quiet, shy child.

Being Alone Versus Loneliness

Jan was reading the kid's bedtime stories in his usual animated voice while she was doing the dishes. The giggles erupting from the room made her smile. Dreamily, she gazed through the window onto their back garden, thinking he was so good at some things, but why could he never make a loving gesture to her? Never just hugged her without the compulsion to fondle her, never even showing any interest in her thoughts or feelings? She always asked how his day had been.

"One more...Daddy, please..."

"You two go and read the rest yourselves. Sonja, I know you can. Read to jour brother so that he can follow your reading words."

The kids still shared a bedroom because Jan's parents were expected to visit for the first time. Her in-laws had never travelled away from Holland, unlike her parents. They were very religious, so she was somewhat apprehensive about how they would take to her New Age attraction, as Jan called it.

Regular Routines

The days turned into weeks. Would that be their daily routine now? Serving as the dutiful housewife for him? How would she explain why she had cut up all her cigarettes? Jan hadn't asked again, and he might never do so, knowing him. Her intuition told her to say nothing until he asked again, but she knew she was eager to share her experience, knowing that his response could hurt her.

"Are you baking something?" Jan called out from the lounge. He knew she only baked on Saturday. He wanted his coffee.

The TV in the lounge was turned on at eight, so it was coffee time. She and the kids were very well-trained. When Daddy watched the news, they were never to interrupt. She knew that he was preparing his pipe by now, and she waited.

Automatically, she prepared two mugs of coffee because her disappointment lingered, thinking back to his response when he came home from work. She was often on automatic pilot mode when she felt hurt or sad. After Jan had changed into his gardening gear in their bedroom and walked into the kitchen, she asked him if he liked his work and the people he worked with. He never replied but wanted to get into his garden right away. That was when he must have seen her cut up her cigarettes in the barbeque.

The Lonely Evenings

"There you are. Why were you so long in the kitchen, woman?" The aroma of his pipe made her immediately crave a cigarette, but the idea alone made her feel ill.

"Why are you in such a hurry?" Noticing that the TV was turned off. "Is there nothing more to watch?'

After the news, she more or less could choose what to watch. Jan was not interested in sports; he only sometimes watched documentaries, and they both started to watch Dallas. She hoped that there was a movie to watch. He knew that.

TV was not the main entertainment focus in their lives. Sometimes, the kids watch a children's program after they have done their homework. The TV was never on during the day. In Australia, she sometimes watched a movie during the day when Jan was not home and her babies were playing in the playpen. It was more about ignoring the inner loneliness of not having anyone to talk to.

Now, she started to dread the evenings. She wished she could work on her leatherwork in her outside room, but the light from the one ceiling bulb was not good enough. Watching a movie took her away from her feelings; if they watched them together, she felt more connected to Jan.

Lack of Communication

"Is there nothing on the TV?" she asked again

"No idea."

They were drinking coffee there, and there was nothing else to discuss. Her latest paper bag from Pam's second-hand shop was waiting for her, but she would rather talk.

"What, not smoking?" he asked.

"No, I told you I quit." She wished she could still play a music record, but they had sold their turn table and all their music in Australia before they left.

"Maybe we should get a music player again. I miss listening to music."

Jan got up to turn the small transistor radio she had used alone in Durban. The classical music filled their lounge.

"Are you now telling me what made you quit smoking?"

Her heart skipped a beat because he asked. Where to start? How was she going to explain the voice?

"Somebody told me to stop smoking; something to do with me not 'growing' if I kept smoking."

"Oh, what do you mean by not growing?"

"I was not sure myself, but I now think it had to do with my mind. I would mentally not grow."

"Who told you all that nonsense? You are reading too many New Age books!"

How could she now admit that it was a voice she had heard? He would blame her hallucinations on the books she was reading. She had read about channelling but was sure she had experienced the real thing.

Sonja's budgie was twittering from under the cover draped over his cage. The kitten Tweetie jumped on the backrest of Jan's chair to be nearer its cage. Jan laughed at the kitten's hunting pose, but she was more worried that their new pet would one day jump onto the budgie cage.

"Better get her down and read your book about what, warships? Since you believe that everything I read is nonsense."

"Why not get into bed and have sex? Come, let's make an early night." Jan emptied his pipe and got up. It was just after nine, far too early for her. She was far keener to get stuck in a pocketbook by Marshall Gardner, which Pat said was a fascinating read. It was about the possibility that their planet Earth might be hollow. She would love to inspire Jan to read it since it was not like a spiritual book.

"You go. I will read my book first. It's far too early for me." She knew it would annoy him, but she was not in the mood for sex. Was she ever?

"Grrrr, you are boring," Jan said, smirking as he picked up her pocketbook. His whole behaviour made her feel sad. They had been married for nearly eight years and seemed to have nothing in common anymore. Had they ever? She now wondered. Jan was reading the back cover, and she was still hoping he might be interested. Inwardly, she hoped he would stay and talk.

"What a lot of rubbish...the Hollow Earth. Woman, get to your senses and come to bed."

She curled up on the couch and grabbed her book from him, "I'm not boring; I'm just not in the mood. I miss having a stimulating conversation, but all you want to do is have sex and go to sleep. That is boring!" So she had finally said it!

She tried to ignore him by pretending to read while feeling hurt by his degrading tone. It was the first time that she rebelled by not going to bed at the same time. She truly hoped he would be fast asleep when she joined him. Was this the beginning of their breaking up?

The author concluded that there was evidence of an underground race of serpent people living inside the Earth. She wondered if the novelist Jules Verne had speculated on the same idea but created a fictional story about the possibility, considering that the atmosphere can harbour life deep beneath the Earth's surface.

She was glad Jan had not started reading this book because he would laugh at what he would call an incredible idea.

Hopefully, he was asleep because she had been reading for over an hour. Tomorrow, she would carry on by reading a diary written by Byrd during his polar flight.

Chapter Two

Feeling Discontent

She had to find ways to get rid of the depressed feelings that lately seemed to hang around her like sticky glue. She needed to see people or visit friends. More than ever, did she miss her own family, but what could they do about it? Her mom would always share her own relationship stories instead of listening. She would end up listening to her dramas. Her dad would listen and probably admit that he never thought Jan was the right partner for her. She always knew his thoughts about their marriage, which wouldn't solve anything. Her sister lived a different life, and they had nothing in common.

It was ten O'clock on a windy morning. The house was tidy, dishes were done, and washing was on the line. Jan had gone to work, and the kids were at school. Lately, visiting her friends for morning coffee instead of doing her leather work has become more and more attractive.

Taking off from Leatherwork

When they were still in Durban, some of the mothers whose children went to the same pre-school as Sonja dropped in for coffee, often unannounced, and that was okay when she was working in her garage. Now that they were in Port Elizabeth, Jenny or Marisa, immigrants from the UK would often visit her after they had dropped their kids at school and done their shopping. Then, she had to stop working in her outside room and sit in her lounge to be social.

Deep from within, there was a kind of boredom. What she wanted to discuss with others was outrageous, too far removed from their interest. Instead, she became robotic-like, knowing how to interact with them. Their thinking was aligned with what they spoke about, so she had to admit she was kind of a fake, which she disliked so much in others as a small child. She had always known when people's thoughts did not reflect their words; now, she did the same.

That was why she often felt like leaving the house to visit them instead. Being away from her own home made it somehow easier to interact with others and was less boring.

A week later, as she drove out of their driveway, she spotted a woman cleaning the front window next door. She had not yet introduced herself to her new neighbour, and she knew why. Finding Jan in an embrace with the previous neighbour weeks ago, when she had come home early on a Saturday because the gemstone club was closed, was still a painful memory.

When she drove past, she knew the woman had seen her, so she waved. It was not fair to be unfriendly just because of what had happened. She had never told her friends about it. She hated sharing her marital relationship with outsiders.

Jenny and Marisa lived on the other side of the freeway in a newer suburb than theirs. Both their husbands worked for the motor industry.

Jenny was not home, so she figured she must be at Marisa's around the corner.

Housewives get Together

"Hi, there. I was going to phone you!" Marisa said the moment she opened her front door.

"I must have sensed you were holding a coffee party." Marisa's youngest, a boy of four, was playing with his big truck on a high-piled rug in the centre of the lounge.

"Did you read the paper about the woman who found a way to make international phone calls for free from a call box?" Marisa asked, showing her the newspaper clipping Jenny had brought along.

"Really. How? I have never seen it, but I don't read newspapers, and Jan has said nothing about it. "She was surprised that the article in the paper would describe how she did it in detail.

She looked up because they were both waiting for her to say something. "Let me guess, you both want to try it out."

"Don't you?"

"Not from my phone at home. Just now, Telkom gets wind of it. "She wondered if the woman had been caught and then told a reporter about it. She imagined chatting to her mom and sister over the phone for FREE! They only ever phoned them for their birthdays because international calls were costly.

"There is a phone booth at the shopping centre; why don't we try tonight when the men are home? " Jenny suggested.

"Mmm, I'm intrigued; let me reread it." She went over the details again, knowing that Jan would disapprove! He was a real stickler when breaking rules unless they were his own.

Jenny had baked scones, telling her it was her turn to bring something for the coffee next time. Marisa was openly moaning about her hubby not being interested in their sex life.

"He always complains that he is too tired. He knows I want to try to fall pregnant again."

Jenny laughed at Marisa's plan to seduce her man, so she felt even less tempted to share her relationship issues. Jenny offered her a cigarette and was surprised that she declined.

"Gosh, you are serious! Really! Did you stop smoking? I'm impressed." Jenny remarked. Marisa wanted to know the real reasons since they knew that Jan smoked a pipe, so it could not be because of him. Jenny's husband hated her smoking, but she told them all that it had to be her decision and not his. That would never work.

Her intuition told her not to share the real reasons, so instead, she chatted about how funny her mom would react to her suddenly phoning her. They planned to get together after supper in the evening when the kids were all in bed.

A shift in her Outlook on Life

During her drive home, she wondered if it was perhaps not all her fault that Jan was so irritated at her. There was no time to visit Pat at her bookshop because the kids would be home soon, and she wanted to start preparing a new leather project for her afternoon leather class next week at the college. When she stopped at the traffic lights, Hendrika wondered what it would be like if Jan was not interested in lovemaking. Would she feel hurt about that? Marisa was frustrated because she wanted to fall pregnant, but was she feeling hurt? She had wanted to ask but felt that might have been too personal.

Having a third baby was no longer an option for her. Two months previous, just after her parent's visit, Jan had made sure that wouldn't happen by having a vasectomy without consulting her about it. At the time, she felt outraged that he had gone and had that done without asking her first. She now wondered if another baby would have improved their relationship. Jan hated seeing her pregnant.

When she drove into their street, she saw both Sonja and Lucas in the distance walking home from school. She was just in time.

"Mama, did you buy seeds for Tweetie?" Sonja asked the moment she walked inside. She had run out of time for shopping and had forgotten about buying pet food.

"I waited for you both to get home so we can go together." She lied because she wanted to find out where the phone booth was. She had never spotted it before. While the kids were in the pet shop, she might also have taken the chance to pee in Pat's bookshop. Maybe she had books on relationships. Otherwise, the library was another option.

Arriving Home Together

"Mommy, Daddy is home." Both kids were out of the car before the engine had been turned off. Jan had parked next to the garage. That meant he would leave for work later.

"Hi there. Are you going back to work tonight?" Jan was making coffee in the kitchen, asking if she wanted some. She kissed him as if last night when she spoke her mind had never happened and unpacked the groceries. Jan smiled while preparing his pipe. Before preparing supper, she used to join him and light a cigarette, but now she only accepts her coffee. The voice that told her to stop smoking was still ringing in her inner head. Who had spoken those words? Oh, if she could only share her mystical experience with someone.

"No, I'm free, but we have been invited to a braai just now, so I'm sure I will have to get some meat." She was amazed. It was a weekday, and she had not prepared anything.

"Who invited us?"

"Our new neighbours, I will get some braai meat now. That is why I left my car outside."

All she could think about was that trying to phone her mom from a phone booth illegally was out for tonight unless they came home early, and Jan would tuck the kids in bed. Somehow, she needed to phone Jenny or Marisa to ask if it was too late for them to go out after eight.

When Jan had gone to get the meat, she quickly phoned. Marisa had already arranged with Jenny to meet at the phone booth around the corner from Pat's bookshop just after eight. If she were not there, they would give it a try anyway.

She hoped their new neighbours were a nice couple and not anything like the trashy woman Jan seemed to have had a liking for. His taste in women was nothing like hers but more like ordinary women who flirted with him.

Getting to know the New Neighbours

Her new neighbour Judy, an Afrikaans mother of two, was friendly enough, but the first thing she saw was her terrible complexion. How horrible that acne could leave such marks. Sadly, during the braai, she talked about illnesses. Her two boys looked healthy enough but were older than Lucas by three years or more, so they ignored them both. It must have been the language because they only spoke Afrikaans, as did Mike, her short, podgy husband, who tried to engage Jan in conversation about rugby. They never followed the Springboks, a South African rugby team, on TV, and Jan's pipe-smoking seemed to have bothered Judy. She kept coughing, even outside.

"Do you like speaking Afrikaans?" she asked Jan when they returned home. He was carrying Lucas, who was fast asleep by then.

"I speak it every day at work. They are all Afrikaans speaking except for you know who." He meant his Dutch colleague who had lived and sailed on Lake Malawi.

"Mommy, I do not like these boys. They never ask Lucas and me to play with them."

"Did you speak Afrikaans or English to them?"

"English, as we speak at school, they do not understand when we speak Dutch, and I do not like speaking Afrikaans." She said it with such an arrogant tone; where had she picked that up from? It was Sonja's turn to sleep on the top bunk bed, which was just as well. Lucas never woke up when she changed him into his pyjamas. He was feeling warm. She wondered if he had a temperature.

"Jan, what do you think?" Lucas was a sickly child, but she didn't want to be like her new neighbour, talking in front of her kids about their ailments. Really!

"He might be fine tomorrow. It's always up and down with him. It's late, so let's go to bed."

"It's only ten o'clock! I want to read my book." She knew that irritated him, but she was wide awake after their visit next door.

Entertaining at Home.

Two weeks later, her new neighbour Judy asked why she had never come around to visit. Judy had visited her several mornings while working in her outside workroom, so she had not bothered, and they had so little in common. Jan had not spoken to her husband again but felt obliged to organise a return braai party in their back garden. Jan Liked holding a barbeque as long as she organised everything. If she asked Jenny and Marisa, along with their husbands and kids, to join them, then Jan would not need to entertain the neighbour's husband. *"Why do you think you're responsible for his behaviours towards others?"* Her inner voice was talking to her as if... were there two of her? That was silly, but inwardly, she knew she was embarrassed by how Jan sometimes was toward others, and he was happy enough looking after the meat.

Overseas Phone Calls

"Jan, do you mind if I visit Jenny after dinner?" He was reading the paper and smoking his pipe in the lounge.

"Not if you do not stay away too long. I might get a phone call from work" The kids were playing in the bath. Jan would read them a story after they had finished. That was still their favourite routine while she cleared the dishes.

"Do you have to go to work tonight?"

"Mommy, Lucas is hitting me!" The noises from the bathroom made them both realize that Sonja was growing up and started to get impatient with her younger brother. They were only two years apart, and Lucas was getting more boisterous.

"Lucas, leave your sister alone. Get dressed, and you can pick the book for Daddy to read." Her seven-year-old boy still looked skinny, and the dark shadows under his big blue eyes kept worrying her as she wrapped him in a large bath towel.

"Where are you going?" Sonja must have seen the car keys in her hand.

"To Aunty Jenny to ask if they want to come for a braai this weekend."

"Will Oliver come too?" Lucas asked.

"Of course, and the new neighbours with their two boys."

That started a whole debate, so she left Jan to deal with it. She wanted to join her two friends at the phone booth near Pat's second-hand bookshop. She hadn't told Jan she would try phoning her sister and mother from a phone booth. Both Jenny and Marisa had done it successfully two weeks ago. They had been chatting to their family in the UK. She truly hoped it still worked with just one coin!

"I'll be back in one hour, I promise." She was driving the Beetle so Jan could leave in his company car in an emergency, but they had never left the kids alone in the house before. Sonja was already eight and a half but far too young to look after her younger brother alone.

Feeling like a Criminal

There were two phone booths. Marisa and Jenny were each chatting inside to their family when she arrived. She waited outside, hoping nobody else needed to use the phone.

"Oh good, we waited for you," Jenny remarked after she hung up. I'll show you what you must do. Give me your mom's phone number."

Her heart was pumping, knowing that what they were doing was grossly illegal. After putting a ten-cent coin into the phone, she watched Jenny force her finger into the dialling wheel quickly every time she dialled the following number. She then listened and winked.

"Here, quick. Someone is picking up."

"Mommy, is that you?" she rattled quickly in Dutch. Her mother was in shock when she recognised it was her.

"What's wrong? What has happened?"

It was stupid of her not to phone her sister first. She should have prepared her mom for her phone call. Now she had to explain why she phoned and why it was from a phone booth. It took a while for her mom to grasp that the call only cost her one coin. She kept asking if everything was okay.

"Mom, I now have to hang up and phone Jolanda."

"They are not at home. Why?" Again, she tried to explain what they were doing, but by now, both Jenny and Marisa were making signs for her to finish the call. They were getting anxious, and so was she. After at least twenty minutes, she only paid ten cents for an overseas call! It had worked! They could not stop giggling when they walked back to their cars.

"And what did your mom say?"

"She kept asking if something was wrong because we never phone them unless it's their birthday."

"Really? You never talk to your mom, not even from your landline?" Marisa asked

"We have a landline because Jan's firm pays for it, so he does not want me to use it, only for emergencies. Knowing his parents did not have a phone, that rule so hurt her.

"How is your brother Marisa? He started his new job, but not so?" She had better change the subject and not talk about her unhappy situation at home.

"Can you believe it? He packed everything up, gave up his flat, enrolled the kids into a new school and moved temporarily in with his wife's parents until they found somewhere to rent. Guess what happened?" Marisa came from a large family. She only had one sister but would have loved to have had brothers.

It was a warm November evening, and Jenny and Marisa came in one car, chatting outside.

"What?" They both replied to Marisa's family dramas

"My brother arrived on the day he was scheduled to start his new job but was told the job was no longer available!" They were both shocked.

"Is that legal? Is that allowed?" she asked. "How can a company do that to anybody?" At that moment, a vision of many people rioting flashed before her eyes as if? ...Something to do with people who all lost their jobs?

"Are you okay?" Jenny asked, resting her hand on her shoulder.

"Yes, sorry, I had a flash...never mind." They chatted and accepted her invitation to accompany their families to the weekend barbeque.

Dealing with Major Disappointments

On her drive home, she thought about how Marisa's story reminded her of their disappointment when they arrived in Melbourne years ago. While living in Holland, when Sonja was a baby, they met Jan's uncle and his wife at his parents' home. They had been on a family visit. His uncle had immigrated to Australia many years ago and lived in Melbourne. He worked for a market gardener company but wanted to start his own, and when Jan told him that they were keen to immigrate to Australia, his uncle immediately wanted them both to join them in Melbourne. He loved starting a market garden business with Jan, his nephew. Gosh, why was the rioting happening in Melbourne? Visions that were suddenly so clear from that one time...why did her thinking of Melbourne trigger them?

She had to grasp the steering wheel to ensure she was fully awake as she entered their street.

Jan was still at home; his car was still parked in the driveway. Gosh, she had completely forgotten about how his uncle had disillusioned Jan. They had been living in Fisherman's Bend Hostel in Port Melbourne for six months while he worked in a nearby factory because the Australian government did not recognise his merchant navy papers. They kept hoping that Jan's uncle was still keen to start a garden business with Jan. Every time they drove to their place for a visit, his uncle no longer spoke about starting his own business. They had arrived in Australia with money, but Jan wanted to invest it in the proposed joint market garden business.

When it became clear that his uncle had changed his mind, they bought a house, and Jan started a house painting business with someone else. He hated every moment of it. Jan never expressed his hurt, but she knew his uncle had hurt him. During their four years there, she was never allowed to tell her uncle why they had come to Melbourne because Jan felt it was his mistake to believe in him.

In her heart, she felt sorry for Jan because he bottled up his feelings. When she entered the lounge, she hugged and kissed him. "Hi, there. Have you already made coffee?"

"No, I waited for you. Did you ask your friends for a braai?" For the first time, she became aware of the strong smell of his pipe tobacco in the room.

"Yes, they are coming Saturday around five. I'm glad you do not have to go to work tonight. After coffee, I will take a long soak in the bath and then let's go to bed."

That was the first time she had mentioned the going to bed part. She had looked at Jan from a different perception. He was a good man whom she could rely upon.

Chapter Three

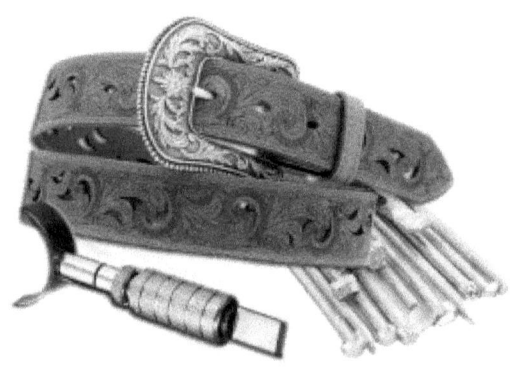

Leatherwork & Art

Working away at her leatherwork in the outside room made her always feel good. The summer had truly arrived, and her once-a-month Art-in-the-park market was getting busy.

Somehow, she wanted to express her searching mind in a more image-driven way. Maybe she should return to her drawings or take up painting again. Several creative ideas came to her while hammering away at belts for Art in the Park. After her belts were done, she needed to do some airbrushing work. Her African designs on leather were taking off. Every month, she sold at least one leather wall hanging in addition to the usual belts, purses, and other items from her unusual gift lines. Lately, she has been looking for different projects from what other leatherwork stallholders made.

"Are you coming in, or do you want me to bring your coffee here." Gosh, was it already that late?

"No, I will join you in the lounge. Sorry, I got carried away." She felt grimy and was looking forward to a long soak in the bath while reading the book by T Lobsang Rampa that Pat had kept for her. The doctor from Lhasawas printed it long ago. She was fascinated by Lobsang's story, which continued with him living in Chungking, China.

Bath Rituals

Jan never took a bath, and now he had renovated the bathroom by adding a shower. The bath was far too short for him anyway since he was over six feet. On the other hand, she loved treating herself to a glass of wine and nibbling while reading her book. There was nothing to watch on the TV, but it was just after nine, and it was far too early to go to bed.

"I'm going to take a bath." She said wearily

"Terrific. Is that an invitation for me to join you?"

"Oh, you hate bathing, and I'm cold. I want to lie in hot water and read my book."

"OK, I'll clean up."

She felt guilty that she could barely bring herself to suggest the going to bed part. Instead, she hoped Jan would be fast asleep when her bathwater cooled off.

Jan came in and sat on the edge of the bath, feeling his eyes roving all over her while she tried to keep reading. She didn't feel she could reject him, and by the time she joined him in bed, she knew they would have sex. She didn't want that but went through the motions, hoping it would be over quickly. Jan would never inquire if she enjoyed sex. He said once that they maybe should do something different, but she was put off when it became clear what he meant.

It was a strange feeling; her mind was so distant from her actions. After it was all over, she closed her eyes, and it felt like she was floating above herself, detached from Jan, looking down at them both. Jan was already fast asleep. The feeling was always the same: gooseflesh all over while she moved away from her body.

The sensation was like she was getting smaller and floating like a void with nothing. The moment she would look back down, it was always the same: she would fall into her pillow as if she had come from a great height.

Going Shopping

Jan had no ships to attend to this Saturday, so they planned to hold a barbeque in the back garden for the neighbours and friends later in the day. Jan loved cooking in the backyard, so going to the drive-in was out for this evening. Their new neighbours were bringing Potjie Kos. She was not all that fond of a stew cooked in a three-legged cast-iron pot over the open fire, but the men all loved it. Jan had given her a shopping list.

"Mommy is going shopping; who wants to come along?"

"Can we go past the pet shop?" Sonja asked

"We could, but I must warn you two, no more pets, no matter how cute they are."

"I'm staying with Daddy while he makes a fire." Lucas decided.

Wow, this was the first time the girls would shop without the men. They had two hours to buy stuff for the barbeque, so she had an idea. There was a new clothing shop she had spotted last week next to the coffee shop. She would make their shopping a girl's outing but kept it to herself.

On the way, she told Sonja she planned to park across from the pet shop and leave her there.

She would quickly go into the supermarket to buy boerewors (spicy sausage), lamb chops, chicken for her kebabs and wine. Sadly, there was no time to pop into Pat's second-hand bookshop.

Being Flirted At

After dropping all the groceries in the boot, she looked through the pet shop window and saw that Sonja was helping the shop owner feed the fish.

"Mom, look"

A rugged but good-looking man about her age held Sonja up high so she could sprinkle fish food into the large aquarium holding tropical fish of all colours.

"Tell your mom what I told you about the fish." He said, putting her down. He looked her over and winked. She could feel herself blushing. Sonja was babbling on about how to keep fish, and it became clear to her that the new owner of the pet shop had a passion for tropical fish and was trying to inspire her girl to start a new hobby.

"Sonja, next time, we will spend more time looking at all the beautiful fish, but we now do not have that much time left. Daddy is waiting for the meat." The man kept flirting with her, but hearing that a daddy was waiting for them seemed to have broken the spell. New customers took his attention away.

"Come, let's go and browse for some nice tops for us both, and then we'll have an ice cream next door. How is that? Just us girls."

"Yippy, can I choose?" Sonja's new fish hobby had slipped her mind completely. It was amusing to be shopping with her not-so-little girl anymore. They walked out with T-shirts and some bangles made from African beads.

Keeping a Secret

Jan took the meat out of the boot the moment she arrived home. He liked to marinate it for at least half an hour before cooking. They were both in the kitchen having a glass of wine while she prepared the salads and the kebabs.

"I'm sure we have far too much food. They will all bring their meat as well." She commented when the front doorbell announced that people had begun to arrive.

The kids ran to let them in, especially greeting the children. Sonja was already wearing her new T-shirt.

"Jan, what do you think about our women having the time of their lives phoning home from a phone booth?" said one of the quests. Jan's expression was full of puzzlement.

She had never told Jan because she knew he would disapprove. Jan had no time to ask her about it because both husbands had already explained how they had tried it out. Thank goodness that by the time the Afrikaans neighbours arrived carrying the cast iron pot, the phone booth adventures had done their round. Barbeque recipes were now being exchanged.

After her first free phone call from the call box to her mom and sister, they went twice, but to a different phone booth. Just in case the telephone company was getting wind of it. Her last call had been cut short when suddenly a voice interrupted her, saying: "I know what you are doing."

Knowing she had been caught doing something illegal, they had all run away from the phone booth, giggling like naughty schoolgirls just in case a police van would suddenly appear. That was it—no more free phone calls.

Going to the Drive-in

They went to the drive-in on Sunday evening to see the movie 'Grease' with John Travolta and Olivia Newton-John.

Jan never questioned her about the phone booth story anymore, and she was glad, knowing he would not have approved it.

They had been chatting about selling their home in Rowallen Park to look for a home closer to town. The 30 to 40-minute drive each day to the harbour was getting to be a pain, especially during peak hour traffic. She had always been attracted to an older suburb with big trees, so in the New Year, after his parents had been for a visit, they agreed to approach an estate agent.

Chapter Four

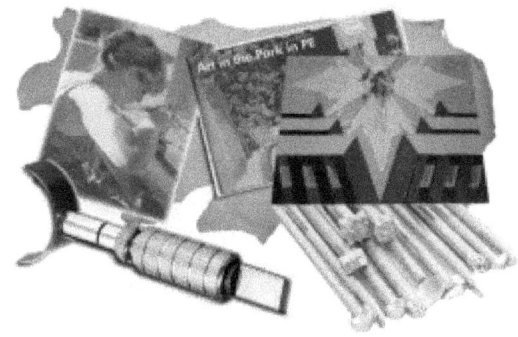

Time was Truly a Mystery.

It had been four years, and she looked it up. Four years ago, they moved into this home in Rowallen Park, and now they both felt a move closer to town would be a good decision. Soon, they would be looking for a high school for Sonja. Lucas would follow two years later.

After Jan's parents visited them in February, they started to look around for the suburbs they wanted to move to. Driving each day into town was a significant issue now that the traffic was getting busier due to the enormous new shopping mall that was being built nearby.

Lately, she has been wondering about how "Time" works. Her vivid dreams seemed timeless, so why did the clock control her waking hours? She was often daydreaming, thinking about life in general. Why was she thinking about life so differently from other people, except for Pat and the people from Cynthia's Yoga group? Every Wednesday morning, it was her day to interact with like-minded people. After their Yoga and coffee session, she would stop by Pat's second-hand bookshop.

She always ensured she was home before the kids were home, but they now had their own key.

Staring out the kitchen window, she realized it would be rainy. She hoped the kids were in the classroom before the drizzle became a downpour. She would drop them in front of the school if it rained. It was not far to walk, ten minutes tops. Jan would be home from work later. There were no Ore ships in the harbour, so he only had to drive to the office, do some paperwork, and then come home again.

Her leather work was calling her, but so was the book about the illusion of time. She got it out of the library, and even Jan had browsed into it the previous night. She always hoped that he would take an interest in alternative ways of thinking, but instead, he seemed to be reading war history books and books about Christian churches, which did not interest her whatsoever. Somehow, she suspected there were a lot of falsehoods preached through religions.

House Hunting

Sunday morning was the best time to write in her diary when she was alone in bed. She had started a dream journal, and lately, a seanery of two mountains ending up in the ocean kept lingering. It was helpful for her to jot down her thoughts and feelings from her dreams, even though her writing was a mix of Dutch and English with many words jumbled up, not to mention her handwriting, which always slanted backwards due to her being left-handed.

The shouting from the kid's bedroom made it clear that the kids were arguing.

Jan had left early to finish an ore ship when the kids were playing in their bedroom. He said he would be back home before lunch.

They were planning to look at some showhouses that afternoon. She loved walking into a show house while the owners were out. Every Sunday from two to five O'clock, real estate agents would sit in homes for sale to show them to prospective buyers. No appointment was necessary, but it was appreciated if one left a name and phone number with the agent. That way, they could contact new prospective buyers. Often, the home was not in their price range, but it gave a good idea of what market value people put onto their property.

Sonja burst into her room without knocking, shouting, "Mommy Lucas stood on my new T-shirt; it's now all dirty", throwing her new top onto the bed. Tears were streaming. A footprint indeed soiled her new top.

"Why was it lying on the floor for him to step on?"

"It wasn't. He did it on purpose." She stamped a foot in anger. Her overreaction was somewhat unusual.

"Calm down. It will wash out." She said and then called Lucas. So much for having some time to herself. Thank goodness for school uniforms. She couldn't imagine what it would be like to have dramas about what to wear each morning as she had over weekends. Sonja knew they were going out in the afternoon, and the weather was mild, but it might rain later.

"Where is Lucas?"

Having sorted Sonja's wardrobe decisions, Lucas appeared to look gloomy. He was guilty, but she wondered why he had committed it. After some debate, it became clear that Lucas felt left out because he had not got new clothes.

"Sonja has always got something new to wear." Good grief, he was right. He hated going into clothing shops, and Sonja loved it, so he was probably losing out.

"Next time, it's your turn to choose a T-shirt, but before you get dressed, say sorry! What you did was mean." She wondered how Jan would have handled it if she had not been there.

Looking at Show Houses

"Can we not just drive to Walmer and see what houses are on show there?"

She loved that suburb, but the houses were often out of their price range. There were three homes in the Sunday paper Jan had brought home, of which one came close to what they could afford, depending on what they could get for their home. What a pity that it had started to drizzle.

"Do we have to go to a different school if we move?" Sonja asked.

She had already found out about schools in Walmer, depending on where they would find a home. Upper Walmer was far more expensive.

"Here it is, the main road just after the eleventh avenue." The flags could be seen and some cars were parked on the expansive front lawn before the property's front wall. Giant trees almost hid the front porch. Instinctively, she knew this home would not be affordable. The advertised price was high, but that did not always mean anything.

"Why are we even looking? The garden is small and too dark due to these large trees." Jan was not interested because of the garden. That was clear.

"Just pretend to be interested. Let's get an idea of what we can buy for the price."

"Forget it. I'm not going inside. I'll wait in the car."

The two girls walked inside while Jan and Lucas remained in the car. All the rooms had a polished woodwork smell. Seeing Sonja staring at the colossal baby grand in the large living room made her recall how she and her sister hated learning to play the old organ at home. A music teacher came every week but gave up in the end.

She liked the place. It had so much character. The agent said the owners were keen to sell and would be open to offers. Somehow, she knew this home would be a good investment, but Jan would never go for it. This property boasts four bedrooms, two bathrooms, a study, and a prime location among spacious homes in Upper Walmer.

"Thanks for showing me around. My husband is looking for a bigger garden with fewer trees." It sounded lame, but what else could she say?

Arguing over Nothing.

"Why did you take so long? We have one hour left to see two more homes" Lucas wanted to see the grand piano Sonja was describing, but Jan drove off. She was feeling hurt by his lack of compromise. What harm would it have done just to have a look?

"I just wanted to see and get ideas. Why can't you go along with it?"

"What for? It's way overpriced." She disagreed. That house had lots of potential. Jan drove, and she directed him toward the lower avenues by following the map.

"Here is the other one. It's a corner plot, and most of the garden is in the front."

"It's a double story. I love it!" There was one other car parked outside the property. This house had a great aesthetic appeal. It was near the lower Walmer avenues, and the price was still higher than Jan was prepared for, but who knows?

"OK, let's look, but don't take too long. I still want to see the last home, which is more in our price range."

She knew that they would never agree on the same home again. It was just like the house they bought in Rowallen Park. She had no say in it; this time would be no different. It seems that they had nothing in common, nothing to talk about, or nothing they liked to do together. All that was left keeping together were the children. Was that normal?

The agent who approached them at the front door was keen to make a sale. He chatted with Jan about what they were looking for while she and the kids looked around. She liked this home's potential, but she had to admit that it would take a lot of money to fix it up. It had been somewhat neglected.

Jan was not interested in going upstairs. He'd seen enough and told the agent what they were looking for. Typical. He never considered what she would like in a home. The agent took the show house boards away when they arrived at the third home. She was glad because the home looked very dull, almost ugly.

Imagine having tyres on the front lawn for garden décor.

Once Upon a Time.

Lately, her day usually began with writing in her diary what she remembered from her dreams. Her diary became a mixed-up summary of what she had tried to recall. She could still see the text she had read in her dream. 'Once upon a time, there was a parallel world which the ancient races on planet Earth knew about'. She blamed it on the books on Egypt she had taken out from the library, but she could never recall that these books spoke about parallel worlds.

"Do you believe in parallel worlds?" she dared to ask Jan as he walked into the bedroom after his shower. To get a response might start a conversation she so yearned for.

"What do you mean by a parallel world?"

He never replied. He was getting dressed in his gardening clothes. This afternoon, they were going to look at showhouses again. The agent of the double story from last week had several homes on his list.

What she had scribbled down in her diary was as follows: This parallel world was a 'mirror image' world which existed directly above the Earth, and to the ancient Egyptians and other races from long ago, it was a genuine place, a divine land they could physically see and point to, especially at night.

"A kind of mirror world where everything is opposite to our world. Something like that."

"That must be science fiction because I never heard about a parallel world. Are you going to get out of bed?" Jan was eager to get to his garden.

"I will, but before you go, have you ever read anything about a giant race on Earth?" she had dreamed about huge, tall people.

"I do not read nonsense. Come, call me when breakfast is ready."

He left her alone to get dressed. They were so drifting apart she wondered if that was normal. The more Jan started to get involved in religious dogma, uttering quotes he believed in, the less she wanted to do with religion.

She promised herself that she would look for books about giants and parallel worlds the next time she visited the library. Her dreams have become more and more futuristic lately, but why did she dream about ancient Egypt?

Driving Into Town

Her Beetle was purring on the freeway into town. Her afternoon leather classes were well attended, and she, like today, sometimes took Lucas with her after she picked him up from school if Sonja had after-school activities. Jan would pick her up later. The ballet was her latest new hobby, but she knew it would not last. Sonja was not as supple as some of the other girls. She had also gone to ballet when she was Sonja's age, but the teacher told her mom that her feet were unsuitable for wearing ballet shoes, so that was the end of her ballet career.

It took her thirty-five minutes to get to the parking bay near the college.

"Mommy, can I finish my coin purse today?" Lucas asked.

"Yes, why not. It's been carved and dyed, but not so?"

Her afternoon leathercraft class was filling up with children and some adults. They were all in different project stages, but she liked helping them all by inspiring them to finish before starting a new leather product. There were three women in this class she was getting to know well.

Wendy, a mother of two little girls still in playschool, joined her classes one evening on a Monday, but sometimes she came in her afternoon classes. Wendy was born in South Africa, but her parents were Dutch immigrants, so she spoke Dutch. She liked herCorry was a tall, slender lady who lived on a smallholding with her husband, a teenage daughter who used to be a model when she was younger, and Ina, a Dutch lady in her sixties.Her husband had joined her evening class. They had invited her and her family to meet Jan and her kids the previous week, but Jan had to work.

"How is the house-hunting going?" Ina, a thin, fragile-looking woman who walked with the help of a stick, asked. Ina still loved learning to create leather products, even at her age.

"We can't seem to settle on the same home, except for the suburb. We would both like to live in Walmer".

The agent for the double-story house that Jan had no interest in a few weeks earlier had been actively pursuing them, knowing that Jan was a keen buyer. He had recently visited Jan's work, telling him what was on the market.

"Jan is keen on a house in the lower avenues, but it holds absolutely no appeal for me. I keep hoping it's been sold." She admitted to the agent since Jan was not home. Being straightforward was a somewhat typical Dutch behaviour.

Chapter Five

Turning Thirty-Two

Her birthday went by without much excitement. Jan had been his usual bland self that morning before driving to work. She secretly hoped for a pleasant surprise, but he had bought woodworking tools she could use! It was her fault. She had been looking for a jigsaw to carve wooden templates for leather class projects, so he bought that.

A week later, on Friday evening, she had prepared supper after coming home from town. Jan suddenly came up with a suggestion, which he rarely did. He proposed a drive-in treat for the following evening. She wondered what had brought that about. It was usually she who made plans to go out..

"Daddy, can we go out to dinner tomorrow before the drive-in? We never went on mommy's birthday?" She was stunned at her daughter's suggestion. True, they never went because Jan had a ship in. She winked at Sonja, who knew her mother was glad she had mentioned it.

"Yes, why not. Duifje, let's look again at that last house just before the agent took away the for sale sign. The agent had come to my office this morning telling me that it was still on the market and they were now desperate to sell, so the price has lowered." He called her Duifje, which made her suspicious. So that was it. Knowing she had not liked that last house, he wanted to get her in a good mood.

"Jan, that home we saw on a Sunday weeks ago looked way too ugly from the front."

"That can be changed as we did with this home."

"No, it's not the same. Our home here had an aesthetic appeal from the start. It was not my first choice either, but money-wise, I suppose it was the best option, not this horrible-looking square box of a home we saw last in Walmer. At least the double story had an appeal, even if it needed a lot of work."

"Forget it. That house was a nightmare from the start, and you know it. We will look and see what can be done to make it more to your liking."

"It sounds to me that you have already been inside. Have you?"

Both children were listening to their arguing, but Jan had already decided. The agent showed Jan the house the day before her birthday, but he had never told her! The hurt he had kept from her was a real downer, but she would not show him how she felt.

The kids were watching TV when she cleared the dishes, thinking that at least moving to Walmer was closer to the college and the Art in the Park venue. Maybe she liked the house inside, and Jan was getting very handy with his woodwork. He seemed to enjoy doing renovations.

Their House was for Sale

The weather was getting more relaxed. Soon, winter will bring more rain. She hoped that it stayed dry for the drive-in later. She was looking forward to seeing at least two good movies after they had dinner out.

"Mommy, can I wear this today?" Sonja had already been dressing up in several outfits, while Lucas needed to be told what to wear. She had better take several jackets and some blankets with them in the car. The sun was still shining behind the clouds, but it was getting windy.

"Let's hope we can still go to the drive-in tonight. You look fine. Lucas, are you ready? Come, daddy is waiting."

She did feel the excitement that they would be out the whole day, first to see the house in Walmer. The agent had made an appointment with the owners at eleven.

When she walked into the hallway, she noticed that the carpet was stank of dog pee, almost making her gag. It was shabby inside, with old-fashioned wallpaper everywhere, and the woman who greeted her looked like she came from a homeless shelter. A grownup son and an older man were watching football on the TV. They never looked up. Jan had fallen in love with the back garden. He had mentioned the size of it.

There was no front garden unless you call old car tyres with a few wilted plants a garden feature. Yes, the price was low even for the lower avenues, but she already knew there was no way she would move in the way it was. Jan knew from her expression that she was unhappy and that he had taken her outside and away from everybody.

"Come on,, forget what it looks like now. We'll put our house on the market, and if we get our price, we can make an offer, and if they take it, we will clean and paint it all, including new carpets."

But the house is so... dull...I'm not too fond of the front. Yes, it has a great back garden, but... The agent came strolling towards them, and she already knew what he would say.

"Shall we have some coffee somewhere and discuss having your house advertised as a show house this coming weekend?"

Estate Agents

When Jan signed the papers, the agent was very optimistic about selling their house quickly. He brought a few couples in the following days. One couple reminded her of four years ago when they met Sophie and Steve, the previous owners, for the first time and how they became friends. Sophie had invited her to join her mother-in-law's yoga class.

Now, she has discovered how a show house worked. They had to leave their home between two and five O'clock. During that time, she had arranged to visit Ina, an older lady from her leather class and her Husband, Kees. They lived in Newton Park.

"Will Tinkle be OK?" Sonja was alarmed when she heard about her decision to lock their kitty in her leather storeroom with all the leather products. Having strangers walking into their homes was somewhat nerve-wracking.

"She is better off. Kitties do not like to be invaded by strangers."

"What about Tweetie the budgie?"

"Nothing will happen when the cage is closed, and we will tell the agent to look after it. OK?"

Visiting Friends

Ina and Kees, a retired couple, made them feel very welcome, and Kees introduced them to a huge Alsatian, a former police dog who, to everyone's amazement, could find a peanut in the grass lawn when it had been thrown like a stick. He would return it and put it in Kees' hand. Lucas was genuinely impressed. Kees had been a dog trainer for the police and loved his work, so he was very good at it.

When they returned after five O'clock, the agent handed Jan a signed offer for their home. It was the price they had asked for, so that was fast. The financial exchange of ownership would be finalized on both houses in three months.

Art In The Park

The kids were at school, and Jan had gone to work, so her time was hers. However, for the last two weeks, she had been spending all her time packing goods in boxes. She was supposed to go to her outside leather workroom to make some stock for Art in the Park, but for the first time, she hoped it would rain on Sunday, so Art in the Park would be postponed to the following Sunday.

Her monthly sales at Art-in-the-park were lucrative, and she almost earned a monthly salary from that day. Gradually, she invented new products, and even her dying technique improved compared to when she started in Durban. She was now saving up for an airbrush to spray delicate layers with it on leather, now that she knew how to mix her spirit dies.

Today she was going to her yoga class for the last time from their old home.

"So, you have purchased a house in Walmer? That is a good move. You will not regret it, I'm sure," Cynthia said. They all agreed when the domestic servant brought in coffee and cake after their yoga session. She wondered how easy it would be to get to her regular yoga morning group after their move. Her Wednesday mornings were a ritual she relied on, especially because she could talk about topics that occupied her mind, and they were always followed by lively discussion.

She would also miss her friend Pat from the second-hand bookshop. It was a long drive from the Walmer suburb near town. She would have to combine a trip with visiting her other friends. How was she ever going to meet new friends with similar interests?

Their yoga teacher, Cynthia, shared with the group that she had been approached to join a training group to become a lifeline counsellor. Sophie, her daughter-in-law, was also interested in joining, and they all thought it would just be something she would be interested in.

"Tell me more."

"What does the training involve?" Sophie asked

"To start with, the training is free, and when the first group has passed an oral exam, we will get a chance to practise on a real phone call and see how we handle it. By then, we have already had many examples of calls to learn what to expect."

She truly respected Sophie's mother-in-law for her kindness and wisdom, so she felt she should at least join her for an introduction meeting in the town near the Art college to find out what it was all about.

Signing up for New Schools

Both Sonja and Lucas were apprehensive about going to a new primary school. There was a dual-medium school she had visited the previous week. Like their last school, they had classes teaching in Afrikaans and English. Her kids were taught in English. All they needed was a set of new school uniforms, an expense she wished she could do without.

The papers were finalised for the Walmer home, and the previous owners were supposed to move out. Nevertheless, they started tearing away all the wallpaper and carpets while the people were still packing.

The kids had great fun helping her tear the paper off the walls, but they were all astonished when the woman asked if they could keep it in one piece so she could use it.

"What are you going to do with the wallpaper?" she asked again while walking past the lounge carrying her stuff to two cars. She was at first shocked at that question. What did she mean? They never saw a removal van.

The house was indeed in a great mess. Not anything like their home. She had a significant cleaning effort for the last few days while piling up boxes for the removal van booked for the following day. When they left their old house for good, it would be clean and empty, but the previous owners of the new house were already two days past their time of moving out and had left it in a shocking state.

Moving into a New Home

Jan had already driven two trips to Walmer to move many of his plants in pots, including the house plants, before the removal van was scheduled to arrive at ten O'clock. He had been doing a considerable painting job after hours two days a row, so she was keen to see what their new house now looked like.

Her leather products and tools were packed in the Beetle with the budgie cage on Sonja's lap while Lucas settled in Jan's station wagon among suitcases with the kitty in a box. They both followed the removal van. It was already well past lunchtime. It was a strange feeling to drive away for the last time.

"Mommy, look"

She saw in her rear-view mirror that a large removal van had arrived just as they drove around the corner towards the freeway.

"They must have been waiting for us to leave." She had not thought that it would have taken them until after lunch before they were on their way. The new owners were from out of town, so they must have arrived the day before and stayed over somewhere.

They had planned to move on a Saturday, so the kids had two days in their new home before going to a new school.

Sonja waved at them, but she was unsure if the new owners, an older Afrikaans couple with a teenage daughter, had spotted it.

"Let's buy a box of Kentucky fried chicken on the way to our new home. I don't feel like cooking on a stove that the owners were supposed to leave behind tonight." She was almost sure that the first thing they had to buy was a new stove on Monday. Jan had not mentioned what the house looked like when they finally were out, but she was prepared for the worst. These people were of a different breed to them. Even the kids called them strange.

They had a new home, a new neighbourhood and new neighbours. It is said that change brings new opportunities, so why did she keep feeling disillusioned?

Settling into their New Home.

No matter how much she cleaned and scrubbed, the old smell of stale energy would not go away. Somehow, this house had not been a happy home. The property had had four different owners before them. That never bothered Jan, but somehow, she kept disliking the house.

The garage was separate from the house with an attached servant's room and toilet but she had one look inside that room and was shocked by the state of it. How anyone could ever have lived there was unbelievable. it had a tiny window looking out over the back garden. The ceilings and walls were black from soot. Someone had lived and cooked in the room. The toilet was even more disgusting, brown and chipped.

"There you are."

"You're home early. Are there no ships?" She had never heard Jan driving up the driveway next to the house. The kids were settling into their new school, and for Jan he was a lot nearer to his work, but she had nowhere to do her leatherwork.

"What a mess."Jan remarked, dragging on his pipe."I'm working tonight."

"I just cannot imagine how anyone could have employed someone and have them stay here. What kind of people were these previous owners? Oh, I'm so hating having to clean this."

"They were not the owners. They were renting it."

"That figures, but the woman behaved as if she was. How are we ever going to change this into my leather room? It's far too dark. We must break out walls and install a big open window."

"Yes, we could do that. I like what you suggested yesterday. Replace the window in the dining room with a glass sliding door so we can walk out onto the back terrace."

"What back terrace? This plot needs a landscaper. I can draw you plenty of ideas if you are interested." She knew the garden was his domain, so any suggestions had to be handled carefully.

The back garden continued forever with a huge avocado tree near the servant's room and a big tree in the centre where white pigeons were nesting. The owner's son had left them behind.

"We could use the dining room window and install it in this room, paint the whole lot and rip out that filthy toilet." She added before Jan could escape inside.

Renovations

It took three months before she could move into her new workroom, but at least she now had more space than ever before. They had ripped out the old kitchen cupboards. Jan was getting very handy, doing most of the woodwork himself to build a new kitchen, and he re-used the old units, making them into storage space, including a work counter for her leather-dying jobs.

The glass sliding door onto the back patio significantly improved, but she still could not grow fond of the house. It had no aesthetic appeal, especially at the front. The other houses in the street were not any better, and making friends with the neighbours was difficult; they were so not their type. She just didn't fit in. Her leatherwork kept her busy, and her Lifeline and Yoga activities, when nobody was home, kept her from becoming a total recluse.

Lifeline.

Her regular lifeline duties were giving her an insight into people who suffer from loneliness and depression. They were often so desperate that they wanted out. She was scheduled to be on a team that went to people's homes when they were threatening suicide. She never asked to be included, feeling rather inadequate to help people who are so desperate, but how could she refuse? It made her look at her own life. Yes, she was not happy inside, but that was her fault. Her non-stop curiosity about life's why, where and when was her own doing.

Yoga Sessions.

Her yoga social group every Wednesday morning was always an outing, not just for the exercise but more about the discussions they had afterwards. She had shared her dreams with them, and Cynthia had lent her a book about dreams. Not that the book described anything she could relate to, but the fact that some authors wrote books about dreams kept telling her that she was not alone in questioning life.

They were chatting about the latest developments at LifeLine. It was clear that Sophie's mother-in-law, Cynthia, wanted to get more involved. She suggested holding their Yoga sessions every two weeks so she could take on more duties. It was a real disappointment, but she was not going to show it.

Sophie and her husband purchased a smallholding out of town to keep horses, which will be far away in the future.

"Gosh, that has always been your dream. I'm so glad for you." She was delighted for her, especially since she and her husband love the same things.

"Yes, we love our new home. It's out in the country, but the kids seemed to have settled in quickly. Mom, what about playing the last Ouija game before we all go our way?" Sophie asked.

"I know why you want to" Cynthia replied, smiling. The housekeeper removed the tea tray to make a place for the board.

"Remember the last time we played?" Sophie asked. "Gosh, it was years ago. I kept asking about my horse that we had to sell before moving into our Rowallen Park home."

"Yes, I do," she replied. "You were truly worried if the new owner would look after her. You kept getting the same reply when you asked if you would ever have horses again. Your horse's name came up all the time."

She recalled Sophie's frustration, saying she had stopped believing in the game. Her own experience had not ever made sense. She had asked if they would ever move away from Port Elizabeth (PE). What else was she going to ask? All she kept getting back was a name no one knew. She never thought about it again.

"Well, guess what! Last week we saw an advert in the Farmer's Weekly about a horse for sale with the same name, and we thought that must be an omen so we bought it...from the paper...and you will never believe it... " Sonja was silent while they were all waiting for the punch line.

"Mom, she arrived yesterday!" They all wondered who had arrived.

"It's my horse! We got her back. The Ouija board was right!"

"That was at least four years ago. Wow! OK, I will ask the same question again because I keep dreaming about mountains, and PE has no mountains."

She truly wanted to ask if she and Jan would be together forever, which made her sad. Nobody knew about the emptiness in her marriage, so why bring that up?

During her drive home, she kept being disappointed. The board must have read all their minds. Those were the letters that were coming up for her... C.l.o.v.e.l.l.y. Nobody knew what these letters meant. Mel said that there was a Clovelly town in England.

"Maybe that is where you are going; who knows?" She somehow did not think so. Instead, she was daydreaming about the visions from a dream about the two mountains ending up in the sea.

A New Family Member

Sonja and Lucas had adjusted to their new primary school and joined scouts. She tried to get Sonja interested in the girl guides, but after two attempts, she gave up. It was not her scene. The scout hall was nearby, and Lucas loved it.

"Mom, can we now have a dog," Sonja asked one afternoon after school.

Lately, she had thought owning a cocker spaniel would be great.

"Let's look at the paper to see if puppies are for sale."

Lo and behold, there were...8 weeks of golden cocker spaniels for R40.- The owners lived thirty minutes' drive away. She phoned the number

"Let's go...before they are gone."

The home was messy, and at least three golden puppies ran and jumped around in the spare room. Two males were already spoken for, so they took the female. She was so adorable. On the way home, they stopped at a pet shop in Walmer and bought a unique bowl and a basket.

"I hope Daddy will like her. What shall we call her?"

"How does Snoopy sound?" She and her sister Jolanda owned a pavement special called Snoopy, and they loved her to bits.

Jan was not all that impressed, but Snoopy was impossible not to like.

Chapter Six

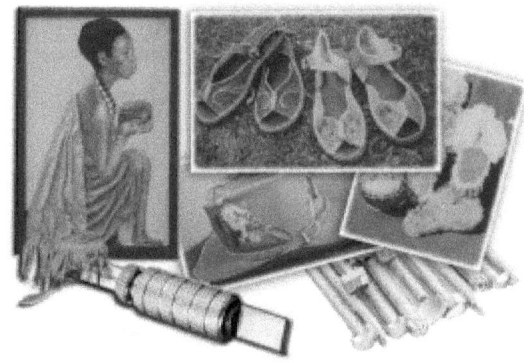

Sonja Enrolled in High School

Life in Walmer took on a different turn. The children were growing up, and she had joined an aerobics class while still teaching at the college, but only in the evenings. They were also planning their first-holiday trip to Holland.

Her little girl was growing up and is now going to high school. It felt only like yesterday when she enrolled them in primary school. Victoria High was within walking distance of their home. Lucas was well-liked in Scouts, and Sonja had joined afternoon acting classes. She was getting involved with designing and painting stage backdrops for their annual play at the Opera House.

Saying Goodbye to a Dear Friend

The traffic was busy on the way to visit her friend Pat from the bookshop. She wanted to get to her as fast as she could. Her husband had told Jan at work that she wanted to see her. She had been diagnosed with emphysema.

The last time she saw Pat she was showing signs of not being at all well, but Pat had always smoked heavily, and she had a smoker's voice, but that it was this bad she could not imagine.

Her son opened their front door, and she was shocked when she walked into their lounge. Pat must have at least lost ten Kilo's (twenty-two pounds).

"I can see by your facial response that I do not look so good," Pat uttered with difficulty. Gosh, her friend was indeed dying. She was attached to an oxygen tank.

"Oh dear, what can I say." All she could do was hug her.

"Well, I'll be on the other side soon... It would truly please me if we could keep in touch..." It took her a moment to digest what she had just said in a whisper...but somehow, it lightened the atmosphere.

"Yes, so would I. Some say they do communicate beyond death." She was thinking about what some authors had written.

"I will give it a go"... her breathing was so shallow...it exhausted her..."I'm ready to go..." oh gosh... she felt her tears running down her cheek from seeing her suffer...

"I've always been glad to have you as a friend," Pat uttered with difficulty, patting her shoulder. Her husband arrived from work, and her son cried, hugging his dad, so she got up and let her family be with her till the end...

Even though she was ready to go, saying goodbye to Pat was hard. During her drive home, the tears made her mascara run. In the driveway at their home, she suddenly knew that Pat had gone...because it felt like she was sitting next to her as a passenger.

Funerals and Goodbyes

When they drove home after Pat's funeral, Jan suggested they take three weeks off from work during the Easter school holidays.

She looked sideways at him, wondering what would come next. " I thought over what you suggested last week, and we can afford it."

"Really! Oh, I would truly love to visit home. Oh, I can't wait to tell the kids. They are both probably at home from school by now."

She had been talking about visiting their family back in Holland for some time now, ever since she had made good monthly money at the Art-in-the-Park exhibition.

"Are you free this weekend? Oh dear, what about Pat dying and all I forgot to tell you?"

"About what? Why is Snoopy outside at the front?" Just then, Lucas followed the puppy as they drove into the driveway.

"What were you going to tell me?" Jan asked, stroking their cocker spaniel, who behaved like they had been away for years.

"We are having visitors for dinner this coming Sunday, Jenny and her family. They wanted to see our home and must tell us that they are also leaving, returning to the UK."

"Oh, what a shame. Yes, the motor industry is laying more and more people off. Shall we have a braai?"

"I already told Jenny that I would make Nasi-Goring."

Lucas was happy to see his school friend from Rowallen Park. It had been a while for them. Jenny's Husband was sad to leave but also relieved. The uncertainty about being made redundant hanging over their heads had started to become stressful for him. Jenny's friend Marisa and her family had emigrated back to the UK after her husband had been laid off from work when they had just moved to Walmer. They had said goodbye to them at the airport nearby.

"Were there lots of people at the funeral, Mom?" Sonja asked. She was doing her homework at the dining room table.

"No, Moppie, just family and a few people who knew Pat from her bookshop. We have something to tell you both." Jan had disappeared into the back garden to water his veggies, so she had to wait to tell them.

"What, Mom?" Lucas asked while rolling on the floor, playing with Snoopy, who was getting increasingly excited.

"Oh dear, let's wait till dinner time. Lucas, why don't you help Dad outside? We will call you both for dinner."

Returning Home for the First Time

Both Sonja and Lucas were very excited about the prospect of their first plane trip to Holland. Easter was soon approaching, and she spoke to both school teachers about their journey, saying they might be a few days late coming back to school.

She was genuinely looking forward to seeing her only sister, Annemarie, who had become a mother of two babies, who would now be toddlers.

She had done a lot of sewing, trying her skills at creating leather jackets, one for herself and one for Jan, for this trip because the weather would be colder.

Holland

Annemarie and Tom, her husband, lived in a modern, freestanding home with their two small children. Their wealthy lifestyle took them by surprise. Her dad had told them about Tom's success in the steel business, but never in detail.

Sonja, her by now twelve-year-old, and she were impressed by how smartly Annemarie' was dressed. Her clothes felt outdated. She had a drastic introduction to the latest fashion during their stay with them.

"Hendrika, I've put some clothes on your bed for you to look at before I give them away."

"Oh really? Gosh, thanks."

"There might be some for Sonja as well, items that are now too small for me."

They were all outside on their wooden deck, having a barbeque Dutch-style under a heater. She knew Jan had nothing in common with Tom, but he tried to make himself useful by preparing the meat and keeping everybody in drinks. She wished to spend time with her sister alone, but her small children were a handful. Annemarie was a great hostess and made them all feel welcome, as was Tom if they ignored his boasting about success. She now understood why her Dad disliked her sister's husband, although he never said it. He was a quiet introvert and a proud man who would never talk about himself or others.

The massive pile of clothes in their bedroom for them to look at was like a dream. Never had she seen such stylish and well-designed outfits. There was nothing that both she and Sonja wanted to leave behind. Sadly, Jan and Lucas lost out, so she bought Lucas the latest hiking gear he could wear to a scout camp back home.

Jan's family was very different and ordinary but very religious. She had to keep quiet and never make 'new age' comments. Her mom was alarmed by her alternative interests and openly said so when visiting her Dad's family in Friesland. They were all very orthodox, with black stockings and all that went with it. Jan seemed to enjoy that, for he often laughed at her mom, knowing it would irritate her.

Visiting Gouda

For their last tourist destination, Annemarie and Tom took them to visit Gouda with her parents. Gouda is a small town known for its cheese. It was more of an educational trip for Sonja and Lucas, but they all had much fun visiting the markets and buying salty drop liquorice to take home. It was there that she noticed how badly Sonja was seeing.

"Can't you read it?"

"No, I do not see any sign; where?"

"What about you, Lucas?"

"You mean the Dutch chemist sign with the medical snakes?"

"Yes, Moppie, when did that start that you do not see so well?" They were all listening, and Sonja was embarrassed by it all.

"Never mind. Before you return to school, we will test your eyes." She sometimes wore glasses to watch movies, but she could see that sign from a distance. How bad was her eyesight?

Saying Goodbye

They were having a late lunch in Amsterdam with the whole family, a treat by Annemarie and Tom when the New Age topic came up. Her mom always told them what the preacher had said, which started getting to her. She had replied with words she should never have responded to. Her sister was the only one who made comments to the contrary.

"Mommy, Hendrika has always heard voices and seen people. We never did." She was so surprised because she didn't remember that at all.

Their flight back to South Africa left around eight in the evening, and she was glad to return home. Their visit back to Holland had been a wonderful experience, but they had grown apart from most family members. She was delighted to be back in South Africa. Somehow, they didn't fit in anymore.

On the plane, even Jan mentioned that he could not see himself living back in Holland again. She was relieved.

Sonja's Eyesight

Sonja had admitted that objects in the distance appeared blurry and out of focus. Her eyesight had deteriorated at a fast rate. Her prescription glasses were now -8. That honestly shocked her since her glasses were only -1. Her new thick lenses were a shame. She was happy that Sonja saw a lot better but was told she would get her contact lenses when her eyes stopped growing.

Lucas's eyes were fine but would have to be rechecked later.

Her eyesight was unusual, so she was told. One eye would see close up very well, but the other would not be as good for distance, like watching TV or driving. She only used her glasses now and then.

Working in her Leather Studio

Her mind wandered elsewhere while hammering away, stamping a pattern into a leather belt. Now that her children were both going to a High School within walking distance from home, she had more time to spend in her workroom in the back garden, creating projects for her afternoon and evening classes at the art college and her monthly show at Art-in-the-Park.

Sometimes, she wondered if a part-time job would not be good for her if she only met more people, but then the jobs that Jan wanted her to apply for were not what she wanted to do.

"Knock, knock," Jan said as he stuck his head around the corner; she was surprised, not expecting him back for hours.

"Hi, back already? It's only eleven o'clock."

There was a silence. Jan came into her workroom while starting a pipe.

"I've been retrenched." She looked up at him, watching his body language.

"What? Really? Why so suddenly? Was that because you took leave?"

"Who knows? They gave me a six-month package, so I'm not worried. What are you busy with?" Jan seemed fine, but she had never seen him emotional about anything.

"I'm preparing belts for Sunday. Now what? Are you going to look for another job in the harbour?" Wondering if he was more upset than he let on. "Come, let's have coffee."

That must have been a horrible feeling for him to be told that his job was no longer there. She stopped working on her belts and, following Jan back into the house; her mind was working overtime and thinking that his loss of work could not have come at a worse time. They had just spent a lot of their savings on an overseas trip!

Jan had already been to the harbour master to fill in forms to apply for an opening as a first officer on the tugs, so he enjoyed spending the rest of the day in the garden.

Job Hunting

She was earning money from Art-in-the-Park sales and evening and afternoon classes, but that was not a stable income. It varied. Jan had posted an advertisement offering himself as a freelance handyman in the local newspaper, but after a few jobs, he did not enjoy it. He didn't find it easy to give quotes for his work.

She had applied to several advertising agencies and made a CV, but after going through some interviews, she knew it would be difficult to find a creative job without an art degree.

"I'm sure you can find an office job." Jan kept telling her.

"I'm not so sure. Don't forget that my English spelling is non-existent, and I have no office experience."

They were both going through the paper's job opportunities in the morning after the kids had left for school. She skipped the sales jobs from 9 to 5. She knew that would never work with her part-time lecturing and leatherwork.

"You do like gardening, so why not consider starting a nursery in our back garden?" she hinted

"That will take years, and then you will need far bigger grounds."

If only he had started to grow plants while he worked so few hours but got paid a full-time salary. Every time they visited a plant nursery over the years she suggested it, but he was just not interested.

The phone rang in the hallway, and both of us had the same thought.

Jan went and came back to tell her that it was for her.

"Who is it?"

"No idea, a guy asking for you."

When she answered the phone, she was told by a man called Paul, who worked from home as an advertising agent, that he had heard she was looking for a job. He was looking for a part-time assistant who could draw.

She was so excited; her interview was for the following morning.

Part-Time Employment.

Her job from nine till two o'clock entailed going to two large department stores and taking back with her the clothes they wanted to promote in the newspaper. Then she had to draw them in greyscale on a transparency paper, and Paul taught her how to use the big PMT image scanner machine that took most of the room in the maid quarters of his house.

After three months of regular weekly payments, lately, when it came to her Friday payday, she was disappointed that Paul had not turned up until well after two o'clock. Weekly paydays became a problem, and Paul's wife seemed to resent her asking for it even as late as the following week, telling her that it had to be paid from her salary!

It took six months after she worked part-time before Jan heard of an opening on the tugboats in the Port Elizabeth harbour, so he applied and go the job. He worked long hours compared to his previous job and hated it.

Walking Out of Her Job

She stuck it out for eight months and left when he had not paid her for over a month. She had learned a great deal about the advertising business and how to do a line drawing for the fashion industry for the newspaper. Still, she might as well do her leatherwork and offer her leather products on consignment to shops. That became a better income in the long run. Being her own boss was far more to her liking.

Time Flies

Jan had done a lot of renovations in their own house when he was off work, and he was getting better with all kinds of builders' work, but now that he was working again, he had less and less free time and often worked weekends, or so she thought.

The station wagon came in handy with all his handyman work. A six-year-old Volkswagen Passat replaced the old Beetle from Durban.

Her volunteer work for Lifeline, Yoga, the stage backdrops and props paintings for Sonja's modelling and drama classes, and helping Sonja and Lucas with school projects between her crafts and housework kept her busy. She only engaged socially with others at Yoga twice a month and during her evening leathercraft classes. She had joined gym classes, feeling that her constant lower back pain must have to do with lack of movement.

She had never met any other friends who were interested in new age topics, apart from the Yoga group, but she kept reading everything she could find at the local library.

Lucas became a Boy Scout leader, and Sonja became increasingly involved in modelling. They were growing up fast.

Snoopy Pregnant for the Third Time.

When Snoopy was a year old, they all decided to get a spaniel companion. Scamper was a pedigree golden cocker spaniel, so they allowed Snoopy to have puppies when she was ready. They had two litters from her, and it was easy to find homes for them. She also earned some pocket money from her babies.

To give Snoopy some rest, the vet gave her a contraceptive injection and they kept them separate when she was on heat, which was not easy.

"Well, that injection did nothing. Soon we will have more puppies to sell" Jan remarked when he came from the back garden into the kitchen.

Scamper mounted her when the dogs were with him in the garden, but Jan did not separate them, thinking she would not fall pregnant.

Shortly before Snoopy was due, they made her comfortable in a big old suitcase without a lid. Both kids were watching over her so as not to miss the birth.

"Mom come, one puppy is out, but it's black."

They were all watching while Snoopy was in labour, and she had three black and three golden puppies. She phoned the vet to ask if the father and mother were golden cocker spaniels. Could they get black spaniel puppies?

"Oh, there must have been another finger in the pie." he replied. She was flabbergasted. She had never known that another dog might have also made her pregnant simultaneously! It must have happened almost simultaneously, but with what dog?

Jan Hated his Job and Wanted to Quit.

After many discussions, she got Jan interested in looking for a plant nursery for sale. They would have to sell their home, but rather that than him hating his work.

They looked at three possibilities, but the prices were too high, and they would have to rent a home. Instead, she decided to open a plant shop where she could give leather classes and offer gift lines. Jan could be preparing potted plants for the retail business; it might work.

The Prickly Pear

Jan had come up with that name, and she had done the window signwriting while he made her shop fittings. Lucas helped by painting the walls after school when he was not on the tug boats.

"Lucas, can you get some more paint rollers from the hardware store across the road so your dad can help you." He had joined them after school by taking a bus to Newton Park, where her shop would soon have an opening day.

Lucas ran out of the front door of the shop. She could see that he was getting tall. Her children were very easy compared to other teenagers who seemed to get into trouble.

Her shop was on a busy street full of shops. Next door was a small bank and a TV repairman on the other side.

She heard a loud screeching sound of a car braking, followed by a soft thump, making her walk out of her shop to see what had happened.

The pedestrians stopped, but she saw nothing and asked what had happened.

"Did you not see that? A young boy was hit when he ran across the road. The van tried to stop, but I'm sure it hit him."

The words "A young boy" hit her in her solar plexus.

Chapter Seven

A Van hits Lucas

"Where is the boy you saw being hit?" she asked several people who had seen the accident.

"Oh, he got up and ran away. Surely he must have been hurt?" a shop assistant from the chemist on the street corner replied.

"Shame. I feel sorry for the driver." Another woman added.

She was at a loss for what to do. Where was Lucas? That is, if it was him. She went inside to carry on working on the display window of what was to become her cactus, plant and flower shop, where she could also do her leatherwork at the little workplace at the back of the shop, which Jan was building for her after he had finished work for the day on the tugs—a job he hated.

A Strange Man

"Are you related to the boy I just hit with my van? A rough-looking man asked her upon entering the front door of the shop. She saw that he was holding a car door, which he had managed to get out of his van.

"I sure hope not. Where is the boy that you hit?"

"Look at my car door; it's all dented. He pointed outside at his van.

"Can you see some fluff from his woollen jersey is stuck there?" She saw it and knew it looked like it could have come from Lucas's jersey that day.

"But...did you see if he was OK?"

"Oh, he must have been. If it was your son who just ran across the road without looking, you are lucky that it is just my work van."

"Was he on the pedestrian crossing?"She knew the man would be more troubled if Lucas crossed the road there.

The man never replied but walked out. Her inner turmoil at the possibility made her nauseous, and she was still shaking from utter shock. About ten minutes later, Lucas casually walked in with a paint roller as if nothing had happened.

"Lucas! Are you okay? Did a van just hit you? Tell me."

"Yes, it was my fault. I was not looking, so I was scared and ran away."

She practically smothered him, touching his shoulder and arms to see if he had been hurt.

"But...I saw the dent...and now I see ...your arm, are you sure you are OK?"

"Yes, mom. Stop worrying. When is Dad coming so we can finish the painting?"

"He said after five, but you know Dad and the shipping industry."

Teaching Leather Work from her Shop

She had to get used to being stuck in a shop the whole day, but at least she could continue teaching her leatherwork skills. Jan had raised the workplace to look into the shop to see if any customers came in.

She had three students for two hours in the morning. They had enrolled in her college evening class, but the shop was closer to their home, so they asked if she would give morning classes.

"If I have customers, I have to see to them, so please carry on June." June was a UK pensioner with a great sense of humour.

Sonja would often take the bus after school. She was already in standard ten and would go to college next year. She loved helping out, and together they would drive home. Her kids were more and more independent. High school did that to them.

Feeling Discontent

Life as a shopkeeper was getting her down. The sales covered the monthly rent and were enough to buy new stock but not much else. She had just enough for some weekend groceries. Somehow, she felt that her life was not going anywhere. Some days, when there were no customers, her mind would dwell on the one unexplained experience years ago. She could not truly address her unhappiness about life. She had two great kids; they were all healthy, and Jan was working even if he hated his job. Her parents would soon visit again for the second time since they lived in Walmer. What or why was she feeling as if she was missing something?

How would she cope with her mother while being stuck in a shop from nine to five?

What sold the most was her sand art gift line in a whisky glass with a succulent.

Family Visits

Her parents came for three weeks, and her mom realised she was unhappy running her shop. She told them that they had been trying to sell their home to buy a plant nursery but without success; even after several show-houses, there were no buyers for their home, so they gave up.

Her dad had been great to have around, but her mom, as usual, had needed a lot of attention.

By the time her parents left, they were both aware that her marriage was in trouble, and the fact that she was so interested in alternative spiritual topics was not helping. Her mom had tried to talk about her relationship by comparing it to her own. She always did that, measuring everything against her situation. She resented that and felt guilty for feeling so irritated with her.

Jan and her mom agreed she should stop reading books on Buddhism, physical phenomena, and literature on UFOs and that Earth might have civilizations inside.

She had to admit that she doubted herself about that possibility, but lately, she has started remembering more details about her dreams. Ever since starting her dream journal, she would recall snippets when she woke up.

Jan's parents had also been for a visit soon after, and spending time in the shop had sometimes been a relief, while Jan was irritated that he had to take leave for a week to entertain his family.

His dad was a bully and not impressed with his son's wife. Her mother-in-law was a sweet lady who took over the household while working. Her mother had never done that. Instead, she tried talking to the neighbours or walking to the shops.

Sunday Morning.

"What are you writing about? It's just past seven in the morning." Jan usually got up before her when he had to work, but today was Sunday. The one day that she was free from the shop.

"Gosh, I had such a funny dream. I need to write it down. I was sitting in the back garden of that Dutch family who lives a few streets higher up in the avenues. You know then from Art-in-the-Park, remember?"

"Mmm, yes, but we have never been to their house, or at least I haven't."

"I know, but I was busy pulling plastic away from my silver necklace in my dream. I was holding my one big ten Gulden silver coin over a flame to melt the plastic away from it."

"Oh, you and your silly dreams. Why not wake me up to have sex instead? That would be a lot more fun than writing in bed." He said in a snide remark when putting on his gardening clothes.

Jan was annoyed as he often was with her. She sensed that he was also not happy but blamed it on her. He didn't like her being so interested in things that he found repellent even to contemplate. She wished they could at least have conversations that were not just about home renovations, work-related or how the children were doing at school. Jan would never join her for PTA evenings; he made sure he had to go to work, but he did want to know all about it afterwards.

They had nothing in common anymore, and now that the children were growing up, they were even less so. Her evening classes at the college or her lifeline duties did not interest him. She always asked about his work, but he never wanted to share anything.

Reading her dream journal was enlightening. Last week, she woke up recalling the same dream of a view over the ocean while in the distance, two mountains ended up in the sea. Sometimes, she awoke from a dream with a feeling of abandonment, being left to get sick and die on the surface of the Earth when the rest of her family were taken to safety in the tunnels below. She had no idea what that meant. Reading her recalled dream again made her question if her mind was not reacting to the book she had just finished about people living inside the Earth.

Going over her notes from a month ago about emotions of grief from losing a child, which was truly nightmarish, made her feel sad.

She had better get dressed and call Jan in from the garden to join them for a full English breakfast. That always lightened his mood.

An airmail letter had arrived letting them know that her parents were planning to come for a visit again the following year. They knew she would be in the shop the whole day, apart from two afternoons in the week when Sophie from her yoga morning would take over.

Jan came in now and then to replace plants with fresh plants from home. She hoped to sell all her fresh Protea flowers and herbs in the wooden wheelbarrow daily.

Life Being a Shop Owner

Being cooped up the whole day reminded her of the milk bar in Australia. Why was her life going the way it was? To admit that she was unhappy was truly silly. Deep down, she had hoped that having her shop would be more fulfilling. Jan kept complaining that the takings were too low and soon she would be bankrupt. Why did he have something negative to say about whatever project she started?

"Hi, Mom, how was your morning?"

It was always great to see her seventeen-year-old daughter walking into the shop. Lucas liked to stay at home after school.

"It was quiet, but I got one good sale of a bonsai arrangement."

"Oh goody, so we can go past the shops to get something nice for tonight?"

"It's Friday, so a cake will be full price, not like on Saturday at noon just before the shop closes, but okay, let's see what they have. Tell your dad that we had a good day money-wise. Otherwise, he will be asking."

"Mom, why does Dad not like what you do? He likes looking after the plants you take home when they have been too long in the shop."

"Dad is not an entrepreneur. He prefers to get a monthly salary to know what he can afford."

"Dad often says you should look for a job instead of working for yourself. I do not understand why he wants you to do something you hate, working in an office. "

"No, he doesn't understand, and that isn't going to happen. I was hoping the shop would bring in more than it does, but it might take a lot longer to establish an income from it. Especially now that I have to use the money to pay Sophie for the two afternoons, replace stock, and pay the rent. I'm learning how expensive it is to keep a shop going."

"Come, let's close up and get something nice to nibble on while watching a movie on the TV tonight."

Jan was working late, so they were a threesome. Defrosting homemade soup and egg on toast would do, knowing that Jan would not be satisfied with it.

Chapter Eight

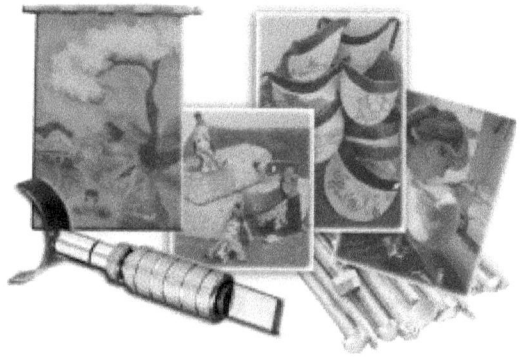

A Surprise Out of the Blue

Her depressed mood, coming home from yet another day at the shop, was suddenly wiped away when she read an airmail letter from her parents. They wanted to buy her an air ticket so she could visit and be with her sister, who was having a difficult time. They never said why.

A break away from home might do the trick. It would help to get her life into perspective if she could see it from a distance and away from home.

They were all in the kitchen. Jan was having a glass of wine, and offered her one as he asked her what they were having for dinner. She handed the letter to him while preparing dinner, hoping he would encourage her to take them up on the offer.

"Well, how can you fly away to Holland for two to three weeks? I do not want them to pay for an airline ticket."

Now Sonja and Lucas both wanted to read the letter. They could read Dutch very well.

"Why not? I can ask Sophie if she would not mind looking after the shop for me. Besides, you do not pay for my ticket; my parents do."

"Dad, I can get to the shop after school if Sophie wants to go home on the days you can pick me up." Sonja offered.

Lucas also offered to go on the days when Sonja could take the bus back home. She was so proud of both her children. Jan had been outnumbered.

After dinner, she phoned Sophie because everything would depend on her willingness to take over full-time while she was away. Her morning leather class students would carry on at home when she returned.

"It's settled. Sophie said yes." Jan was still at the dinner table when she joined them

"So I have no say in the matter."

"No, I will phone Mom and Dad tonight. I also want to know what the matter is with my sister. I know that her premature baby is fine, last I heard."

Later that night, their lovemaking was, from her point of view, more to say thank you for letting her go away for three weeks. Her ticket was booked the next day after her dad paid for it. She would leave in a week, with plenty of time to show Sonja some bookkeeping tricks and buy herself two nice outfits on her Edgars account.

Flying Home by Herself

Her trip to Holland turned out to be a real treat. The weather at the end of April was truly mild, almost warm. Her parents told her what had been happening. Her sister was coping with a tiny baby at home, but she had been through a very traumatic time. While her baby was still in an incubator, she had disappeared for two days from pure shock at first, then hurt, followed by anger. She had discovered that her husband had also been visiting another woman in the same hospital, who was also giving birth to his child. That had crushed Annemarie.

Her sister's marriage had put her relationship in a different light. Annemarie said very little to her cheating husband. They had a dark vibe between them. Inwardly, she was too disgusted for him being unfaithful, and Tom knew that her sister had told her about his affair.

Three weeks flew by. Together with her mom and dad, they visited Jan's parents by taking the train. Her parents did not own a car. They both tried getting a driving license, but her dad failed at least eight times. His measurement of distance on the road compared to a ship was his downfall.

A Decision Had to be Made

She was home for her thirty-eighth birthday, and the breakaway did them all well. She was far more attentive to Jan's needs now that she was comparing her marriage to her sister's, but he was somehow very distant, and most evenings, he came home late.

Since her trip to Holland, being tied to her plant and gift outlet had become even more depressing. Being stuck in a shop was not good for her. There were hardly any customers, and the sales were minimal. How was she ever getting over feelings of utter distress at being there? It had been her choice to own a shop. She had hoped it would improve their relationship now that she could sell his plants and do her leatherwork from there, but nothing had changed.

Yes, Jan did replace plants with others from his tunnel, but he only criticised how little she earned. She still had her evening leatherwork classes at the college and art in the park on Sundays. But that for him was not the same as having a steady job like he had, never mind that it did not make him happy.

Trying to suppress feelings of suspicion that Jan had an affair didn't help. She did not want to become suspicious when nothing was going on.

The trickle of the small fountain below in the shop front inspired her to ask for help.

"Dear God, higher self, please show me how to accept the things I cannot change in others, but may I be shown my purpose. I feel I need to change my direction in life."

The memories of that one time when she heard a voice often made her wonder. She was starting to question if there was such a thing as having a soul purpose.

"Once, I heard a voice that told me to change, but I thought it was an instruction for me to stop smoking. Now I feel that owning this shop was a mistake. Please show me how I can change my life around that will bring me happiness and fulfilment."

Her depression began to lift as if her genuine inner plea had somehow been acknowledged. It was still dead quiet, with no customers, so she closed her eyes again, asking:

"Show me the way and give me the strength to pursue my life's purpose. I trust and hand over what needs to happen."

Never before had she prayed with such intensity as now. It was almost as if she knew that things would change.

This afternoon it was her day off. Sophie would take over, which was already something to look forward to. To have two afternoons off made her realize how much she enjoyed being free to move and go where she felt like.

Be Careful What you Ask For.

She was home when the kids came home from high school. They had to bring Trickle, Sonja's cat, to the vet and do some grocery shopping, so what little money she took from the till had to do, so long as she left enough change for Sophie to work with.

They had three Golden Cocker Spaniels who could escape from the kitchen trap door into the back garden. They left after talking to Sophie on the phone in the hallway about the flower order she had forgotten to mention.

Shopping in Pick n Pay

She was planning to do some leather dying and had already changed into her old jeans before going to the shops. It was a cold, windy winter's day, and Trickle Sonja's budgie was not OK. Sonja and Lucas joined her on the trip to the shop and the vet. Trickle had to stay in the vet hospital for a night. That would be costly but could not be helped.

"There must be a fire nearby," Sonja commented when they walked out of the supermarket and back to the car. Lucas had to buy a cake for school, so she dragged him along. He didn't want to go shopping with his mom and sister, which was not high on his to-do list these days, but she would not be his servant doing shopping for him.

As she drove behind one on the way home, more fire engines sped past when a strange feeling overcame her. She turned into the fourth avenue, which she never did, but seeing the thick black smoke ahead toward their home made her very uneasy.

"Mom, mom. Oh no!" Sonja cried out loud next to the passenger seat.

As they drove nearer to Third Avenue, the shock of seeing the roof of their house collapsing among the flames made her almost lose control of her Volkswagen Passat. The policeman directing the traffic on Third Avenue had to jump out of the way because she drove straight onto the grass verge in front of their home. They jumped out of the Passat in shock.

Two fire engines and an ambulance were parked nearby. Men with hosepipes were trying to control the tall flames coming through what used to be the front window of the lounge. Her heart broke thinking of the budgie cage that used to hang there.

"What have I done?" she asked herself. What had she left plugged in before leaving the house?

"Oh dear God, the Spaniels", She called out. In horror, she looked on as more onlookers crowded around them.

People had now been made aware that she was the owner, but all she wanted to do was get to the back of their property via the side of the house. They stopped her, and one man was running towards her, holding an injection needle!

"I do NOT need that. Please, my dogs," she was now genuinely panicking. Sonja was close to screaming, but Lucas remained silent.

"Mom, look," he said, pointing at a fireman running towards her from behind the burning house in the driveway, holding the budgie cage. Sonja graphed her birdcage. Poor budgie, but he seemed ok. The house she never really liked was gutted.

They were allowed to get to the back garden when the flames were gone. That is where they saw the three spaniels that a strange man was keeping.

"Oh, I'm so grateful they are alive!" She called out. All three of them got down onto the lawn, hugging the dogs. Their eyes were bright red and shaking, but the cuddles calmed them down.

The stranger told her that once before, he had driven past a burning house where a bird was burned alive. A young boy was so grief-stricken when he saw the flames coming out of the roof and the budgie case in front of the window he ran to the back to get into the house no matter what.

It was then that he spotted the three dogs that were trapped inside. He removed the sliding door from the dining room wall and rushed for the budgie case. He was out with the dogs before the roof collapsed.

Due to the crowds of people around them, she never saw the stranger again to thank him for his heroic actions.

Jan, oh gosh, he will be home soon. How would he react?

People in the crowd around them asked where they were going to stay, but all she was worried about was Jan. How was he going to respond to this disaster?

More and more people streamed into the back garden when she spotted Sophie with Cynthia.

They hugged, and Sophie was crying.

"We are alright. They rescued all the animals, and nobody got injured."

"What happened?" Cynthia asked. They had heard on the news about the house in Albert Road, and Sophie had closed the shop to drive with them to find out if they were okay.

People around clearly also wanted to hear the reply. She felt hemmed in by human bodies.

"Oh, Hendrika, I thought you all had died in the fire." Sophie said in a broken voice."I got a phone call in the shop from a woman asking where you were because your house had burned down. I told her she must have been mistaken because I had just spoken to you on the phone."

People in the crowd were all telling others what they speculated about how the fire happened. While she suddenly realized how Sophie must have reacted.

"Gosh, you are right. I phoned you just when we left the house to go shopping to tell you about the flower deliveries."

She needed to calm Sophie down. A tall man called out over the head of the crowd. "When you are ready, we have a room for you all."

She knew him. He was the Dutchman who lived three streets away, near Sixth Avenue.

Suddenly, there was a commotion, and Jan was at her side.

Jan Arrived at a Home that was No More

Jan looked them all over, including the animals. Sonja, still clutching her budgie cage, was shivering from pure shock. Somebody had covered her cage with a towel.

"Well, that is the biggest house cleaning I've ever seen," Jan said in a calm voice; it shook her to her core.

Some man was laughing at that remark, but she wished he was more emotionally demonstrative, like hugging them all to find them alive, but instead, he just seemed to take it in his stride. But was he?

The crowd was by now thinning out. Some still asked where they would go for the evening when she remembered.

"Johan, the Dutch electrician who lives nearby, offered us a room. Remember you met him on one of your repair jobs when you worked for yourself? He was a thin but tall, strong-looking man in his late forties or early fifties. She thought him to be at least over two meters.

"Oh, now that is very nice of him. Where is he?"

"Gone home, I guess." She was now also shivering; it was, after all, mid-winter and none of them had any coats on. It must have been after six by now.

As if someone had heard her thinking simultaneously, she and Sonja were suddenly draped in a blue blanket.

"Oh, thank you so much." Vaguely, she recognized the woman from the house who had backed onto their back garden. No idea what her name was. Lucas was also given the same blanket, but it was folded up.

She encouraged Sophie and her mom to go home and that she would phone them. The shop would just be closed for the rest of the week. There was no way she would cope with worrying about The Prickly Pear, and Sophie needed a break to get over her shock from thinking they had all burned. By this time, the crowds of people had gradually left. The smell from the burning and the smoke was depressing.

Their New Sleeping Arrangements

It took at least a half-hour before the dogs and the budgie in its cage were all bundled into her Volkswagen Passat. Jan had inspected the back garden, but it was getting dark by now. They might as well leave. The fire was out, but the strong smell of smouldering ash still hung around. She drove in the Passat following Jan's new company car.

"Mom, I'm ravenous," Lucas remarked. He had joined her while Sonja was with the dogs and the budgie in the station wagon.

"Let's first go to the people who offered us a room in their home, and then we will see. Probably buy some takeaway."

She stopped next to Jan, who was also parked in front of a house with Dutch lace in the window. He seemed to remember where that Dutch family lived, just a few streets higher up the avenues.

When they both arrived at the front door, a woman came out with her arms outstretched as they exited the car.

"Oh, you poor people, how are you all doing? Come inside; we prepared a room" Her hug was somewhat uneasy as if she did not know how to be around people who had just lost their home.

She now remembered Annie, the Dutch wife from Art-in-the-Park. She had not taken to her because of her bossiness. She seemed to be in charge because she told her where to set up her stall the first time she displayed the leatherwork and sand art she had created in the shop.

The weathered-looking woman, at least ten years older, made her smile and hugged her back.

"I hope you can all fit in there for the night at least."

"Thank you so much. I feel somewhat overwhelmed by your gesture but very grateful, especially for the dogs and the budgie. We could not leave them tonight."

She sensed that Annie had not bargained on three dogs and a bird, but her husband had already taken a rope around two of the dog's collars while Lucas carried the youngest spaniel, who was shivering from fear.

Their Bedroom for the Night

One double and a single bed just fitted in the room. Johan had already put an old blanket for the dogs on the floor.

"Well, you both have to share a bed for tonight." She said to Sonja and Lucas before they thought of complaining.

Suddenly, it hit her. She collapsed on the double bed, still clutching the blue blanket around. What were they going to do? Was their home with all their stuff gone?

Sonja was crying while clutching the budgie cage while Lucas was trying to calm the dogs. Jan was talking to Annie's husband in the kitchen.

The knock on the bedroom door alarmed both dogs. Scamper started barking.

"We have supper ready; please join us," one of the daughters told them from the hallway.

"Mom, the girls are very different", Sonja whispered; I saw their room."

So had she. The whole house was one massive mess. Amazing how some people lived, but she immediately felt guilty for her thoughts.

Adjusting to an Alternative Lifestyle.

Annie, a rather unattractive-looking woman, had made her feel guilty. She tried to warm up to her, knowing that she and the two daughters must have been tidying to make space for them all to sit at the dining room table. When they came in, she was again stunned at the enormous clutter of stuff, especially magazines. The coffee table was piled high with them.

"Both girls cooked for us all; we are so proud of them."

"Michael helped, Mom, and dad." the oldest girl, Janet, remarked timidly as if she feared her mom. Both girls were around the same age as Sonja and Lucas. Teenagers. She went to Janet, who was the best-looking of the two girls. Her sister Lies was podgy with acne.

"Where is Michael? Annie asked Janet

"He took a plate of food to his room outside, Mom." He was an older son she had not yet met.

They had left the dogs and the budgie in the bedroom with the door closed, but now she could hear them scratching at the door. Oh, how embarrassing.

"Mom, I will take the dogs out for a walk. Don't worry, I will eat later."

She knew that Lucas was hungry, but somehow, he had lost his appetite. Lucas asked for one more string to try all three dogs with it around their collar and take them away.

"Gosh, my apologies. They are clearly out of their routine." She remarked while Jan helped himself to potatoes and stew.

Sonja was quiet but suddenly ran away from the table and into the bedroom.

"Oh, dear. I had better go and have a look."

"Maybe leave her," Annie suggested, but she couldn't; her teenage girl was not coping.

Unexpected Arrivals of Goods

"Moppie sweetie, are you okay?" Seeing her girl all tearful, sitting in a heap on the bed, made her take her into her arms, as only a mother could do.

"I can't take my contact lenses out before going to sleep. My kit is gone." Sonja said in a trembling voice.

Oh gosh, she had never thought of that. Sonja had been wearing lenses for a month, and her glasses must have also perished. Oh dear, what now?

"Moppie, I will phone the eye specialist to see if he can come up with something."

They all understood when she returned to the lounge and shared why Sonja had been so upset.

Jan immediately looked in the phone book for his name at home because it was now after eight in the evening. He got hold of the optometrist, and she heard him explaining what had happened and why he had phoned so late. She helped clear the table between the ringing of the front doorbell.

Their dinner was indeed interrupted by all the commotion. Someone had given Johan a closed envelope for them. Included was a check for ten Rand. She had no idea from whom.

"That's nice," Annie remarked as she placed the pudding on the dining room table.

She felt uneasy, feeling Annie's frustration. Strangers had found out they were staying with them and had brought all kinds of stuff.

"The optometrist had said he would bring a kit for the lenses." Jan shared as he sat down, helping himself to pudding.

"Well, that will cost you," Johan remarked.

Money had not been forward in her mind, but after his comment, more and more misery piled up for her. The little money in her bank account would go nowhere, and she had no idea if Jan had any savings. He was always very secretive about his finances.

The doorbell rang again, and someone left a box at the front door and left."

Inside the box was a card that said: we hope this will help you.

When she saw the clothing and even some toiletries, she started to cry. It now truly sank in what they were facing. They lost everything in the house: photos, books, artwork....

Their First Night after the Fire.

Two more people left parcels that same night when the doorbell rang again at eleven after they had cleared the dining room table and were drinking coffee in the lounge. Annie was now getting upset. Johan took her into the kitchen to calm her down. The two girls had gone to their bedroom; they didn't know how to talk to Sonja or Lucas.

She opened the front door and recognized the optometrist—a good-looking man in his late twenties.

"We are so shocked to hear about the fire. I've looked up your daughter's subscription, and here is a kit and some extra lenses that will keep her in stock for well over a month."

All she was thinking about was the cost. How were they going to pay him?

He stopped her when she was about to ask what they owned him.

"Please accept this as a gift. We have no idea what you must be going through, so please do not worry about the cost. Not now."

Her emotions were so charged up that no words seemed right about her gratitude. All she knew and felt was that people were genuinely loving and kind to each other in times of need.

Sonja was very relieved to take her lenses out. They would have to get her a new pair of glasses in between, but she seemed to be OK with just the lenses for now.

That night, nobody could sleep and the pong that the three dogs left in the small bedroom made her get up and sit in the lounge until it got light. Their lives would never be the same again after their house burned down. Everything in their lives had changed. Had she honestly asked for that?

The Day After the Fire

How does one cope when all one's material possessions are gone? How do you regain lost papers, passports, birth certificates and diplomas? You start over again!

She was stiff from the cold but finally fell asleep in the cluttered lounge when one of the spaniels started licking her face.

"Oh, Scamper no!"

"Nobody was up yet, so somebody must have left their bedroom door open so the dog could get out," Lucas whispered.

"Mom, are you ok?"

"Hi, Lucas, yes, but cold. Please bring me one of the blankets we were given yesterday."

"Do we have to go to school today?"

"What time is it?"

"Just after seven. Sonja had been crying the whole night. I couldn't sleep."

"Sweetie, just bring me a blanket, and then we must plan what to do today. Shopping, I guess."

She couldn't even brush her teeth, so she never minded putting on fresh underwear and clothes. She was still wearing the old pair of jeans and a top she usually did the leatherwork on, and she knew that no clean clothes were left on the washing line.

She heard noises made by the family coming from the kitchen when Lucas came back with a blanket.

Taking Each Day at a Time.

After breakfast with Annie and their two girls, they left for high school. Both Johan and Jan had already left for work. She felt down that Jan had never said anything to her when she got out of bed and went to the lounge last night, and there was not even a word before he left for work.

She helped Annie clear the kitchen, telling her she would drop Lucas off at the burned-down home with the three dogs. The garage was still standing, and so was the leather workroom. Both buildings were separate from the main house.

Their Temporary Home.

The contents of the few boxes people had kindly left for them last night were spread out on the double bed. She was grateful for the clothes and could see herself wearing them around the house; she couldn't see herself in them at her shop all day. Sonja had nothing to wear because she only had her school uniform. She was still dressed in the same clothes as yesterday.

"Sonja, let's go. We are going to do some shopping."

Taking kids to school and opening her shop would have to be put on hold. First, a complete change of clothing had to be purchased from her clothing account, and she hoped there was enough credit left. She would get something for Jan and Lucas as well and drive back to what used to be their home. Lucas was taking the dogs to their garage, where usually the station wagon they then owned was parked inside. Jan had already gone to work, so Lucas would be by himself.

Thank goodness for Jan's company car. Jan's station wagon had been given to their Dutch friends who had been staying with them for a week just before the fire. She wondered if they knew about their home being burned down. Thank goodness that they had left to move into a flat nearby. Otherwise, they would have lost all their possessions as well.

. Going Shopping for New Clothes

Walking into the department store in her work clothes with not a lick of makeup made her feel unkempt and dirty.

"Can I choose what I want?"

"That depends on the cost, Moppie, but sure, let's make today a new beginning. I'm sure everything will work out."

Sonja needed cheering up. They were all alive; somehow, living from day to day was their only option. She had some savings, and she was sure Jan had money in his account, but she had no idea how much.

"Mommy, how long are we going to live here?" Sonja whispered in the changing rooms.

"We will have to see. We must first meet up with the insurance agent at the house," which was no longer available.

"Oh, why?"

"Janet's mother told me that Daddy got a phone call early in the morning before he left for work. They found out where we were staying. Tonight, we will discuss our next move. Come, let's go."

Proof of Identity.

They were stocked up four hours later with some essentials for a few days. The most embarrassing moment was when a shop assistant asked her for her identity. Her passport and all other identification papers had been lost in the fire.

"Oh, I heard that before?" the girl at the till remarked.

The bank statement in her bag got her past the security issues. Explaining that her house had burned down was an uphill battle, but after some phone calls to the assistant's supervisor, she was given a temporary allowance.

Sonja got herself an outfit and shoes. They both changed at a coffee shop before driving to the plot that used to be their home.

Arriving at the gutted home where only the wall outside their bedroom courtyard was still standing was depressing.

Chapter Nine

Looters at Their Burned Down Home

"Dad's car is there."

People walked over the rubble, looking for something where their front door and hallway used to be, which made her mad.

"Excuse me, but who are you?" she shouted through the open window of her car.

"Oh, we are just looking." One man replied.

"Looking for what? This used to be our front door, but this is still private property." her temperament was now clearly on the warpath.

"Oh, oh. Sorry. Are you the owners?"

"Yes, and will you please leave." Her voice trembled from anger when she saw his son still picking through the rubble further into the property. At that moment, Jan came walking at a fast pace toward them from the back of the ruined house, chasing more people off the rubble.

He shouted and used foul language. She had never seen him so angry at total strangers.

"You stay here while I get some red paint! When I arrived, people were loading up plants from the back garden tunnel. Can you believe it?" He had almost got into a fight.

The dogs came galloping towards them, excited as if nothing had happened.

"Mom, Scamper found cooked chicken and cooked potatoes where the kitchen was," Lucas added, following the dogs.

Looking at the burnt-down house in daylight was still a shock. Some black scorched walls still stood up to a meter high, so it was easy to see the house layout among the roof beams. Cars were still stopping, but one neighbour from across the road chased them to move on.

Treasure Hunt

Jan had returned and painted a rude sign on one front wall telling everybody that trespassing would be dealt with, with a crude skull added for good effect.

He got some bags, and they all started to look through the rubble to see what might still be redeemable.

"Mom, look here."

Lucas was searching for his tin money box and found it. Sonja's bedroom was the worst off. Jan had dug up the stove or what was left of it. She hoped to have some luck searching for what used to be their bedroom for Dutch money she had not yet exchanged, but she could not remember in what container she saved it.

"Mommy, look, what is this?"

A burned-looking lump of metal was buried deep under fallen beams from the roof.

"That is the metal box where all our papers were kept!" Gosh, it was not closed.

Tearing it open revealed all their IDs and passports, all had burned edges to them. Underneath and still in a partly melted plastic folder were all their charred birth certificates. Everything was soaking wet, so the fire brigade had saved something important.

"Come, let's look further. Who knows what more we may find."

What about her jewellery? Near where her night stand used to be, she recognized part of the wooden drawer. Nearly everything was unrecognizable. All she saw were melted plastic blobs, which might have been the boxes in which some of her jewellery had been stored.

"Come, let's put it all in a plastic bag. We will sort it out this evening."

The insurance people came, and all four were interviewed separately. She and the kids told the same story: they had left the home to go shopping.

She could not remember if she had put the stove off, recalling that she had defrosted and deep-fried Samoosas for lunch before they left to go shopping, but she kept that to herself. Jan must have told them that the home was already burned to the level it was when he came home.

"Mom, Henk and Ellie are arriving in our station wagon."

Lucas didn't know they had borrowed their station wagon after losing everything due to going bankrupt. She could see in their faces that they were both in shock.

"Oh, what happened? We drove past but thought we were on the wrong street for the moment. When did this happen? I can't believe it. "Ellie was overwhelmed by the enormity of seeing only a ruin instead of a home they had stayed in just for a week. Henk was talking to Jan in the back garden.

"Oh, Hendrika, what are you going to do now?" Why did this happen? To you of all people."

They were both standing at what was once their front door. It was an uncanny experience seeing only the outlay of what was at one time their lounge, kitchen and bedrooms. What used to be their home was rather distressing, even if she never liked it.

They talked some more, but their overwhelming situation did not completely sink in. What were they going to do?

Then they left to the house on six Avenue, three streets up in Walmer.

When a Dream Comes True

The weather was mild, so the decision was made to leave the dogs in the garage after they were fed. Lucas had made a bed for them from pieces of cardboard.

"But they cannot get out. There is no trap door for them." Sonja and Lucas were unhappy about that arrangement, but having three dogs in a tiny bedroom was not an option.

"So we have to be back very early to let them out. We can't leave them out in the open; they will follow the car and might not return," she replied

Jan was securing most of the plants in the tunnel and carried outside pots inside the garage. Sadly, only a few leather belt strips were left outside her workroom. None of her large wall hangings or carved leather pictures was found. They had been displayed in the hallways, but all had burned to cinders.

They drove away in Jan's company car, leaving her Passat in the driveway, hoping to discourage people from snooping at night.

Annie and Johan had organized a barbeque outside in the back garden around the pool. It was a mild winter evening. Jan was in his element but still significantly upset at the thievery of people since they helped themselves to pot plants.

She was sorting out the plastic blobs, trying to tear away moulded plastic, when Lucas suggested holding it over a candle flame. It worked. Her silver ten gulden medallion necklace came free, but at the same time, a déjà vu got hold of her.

"Good grief, will you believe it? You dreamt it!" Jan uttered in amazement.

She had, indeed, about a few months ago. She even wrote it in her dream diary.

They all wanted to know if she remembered any other dreams.

For her, the fact that Jan remembered that she told him about her dream made all the difference, and hope was ignited that he would be more open to her other unusual experiences.

Selling the Shop

She had asked her higher self for directions while in the shop, and she got it. The shop took her away from her family, who now needed her more than ever.

She first told Jan about the idea in the bedroom and then during dinner, she announced that she would put the shop on the market.

"You never will sell it," Johan remarked, arousing her emotions somewhat.

"Why not? All I want is what we invested in it."

"People do not buy a gift or plant shops; they start them as you did."

Oh well, she couldn't share that her intuition would lead her to a solution to pay back the loan she had taken out. She had nothing in common with this family but was grateful for their hospitality.

"What are you going to do for money? I mean, you also taught leatherwork from there, right?" Annie asked.

"I haven't thought that far yet."

"Oh, I must mention that a building contractor wants to see us this evening. The bank has chosen him to rebuild the house." Jan announced.

"That is fast." She knew a bank official had asked one evening a week ago if they wanted to sell the plot or rebuild. They wanted to rebuild and stay in the neighbourhood where everybody had been so kind to them.

"In the meantime, we might soon have found a house to rent nearby that will become available at the end of the month," Jan added.

After a few days of staying in their home, they paid Annie and Johan housekeeping money and shared the cooking in the evening. During the day, the children were at school; Jan was at work and would start investigating how to sell the shop. She would not get pessimistic about the fact that there would be no buyer as Johan had predicted.

An Unusual Assignment

She was back in her shop two days after the fire when a very peculiar woman walked in dressed up in a plastic raincoat, sunglasses and a scarf. What was more intriguing was that she had seen her step out of a huge black Mercedes that a uniformed chauffeur drove. There were no other customers, but she stepped down from her leatherwork platform to see what she wanted.

"Someone told me that you might be able to help me repair an Egyptian mummy."

Standing behind her counter, dumbstruck, not knowing what to reply, was a new sensation for her. Was this genuine?

"My son is a collector of ancient artefacts, and during a party at his home, someone dared to stab a genuine 3000-year-old mummy of a young woman. Could you create a leather mask for it to cover her head and fix the cuts in the bandage?

"Well, I have to see the mummy first." She was thinking, let her come up with a real mummy.

The woman turned and walked out to the Mercedes, and low and behold, a few minutes later, the uniformed black man carried a stiff-looking statue into her shop.

"Where do you want me to put it?"

She got into action fast. There was no way this greyish-looking mummy could be seen, so she asked the man to carry it up into her leather workplace, out of everybody's way.

Her creative mind somersaulted into hyper-speed, seeing a leather mould of a woman's head with many long black leather plaits and an Egyptian collar to cover the deep cuts on the centre below the chin area.

"Yes, I can help you, but what will you pay? This is not a normal job." she was now wondering what a reasonable amount was."

"Charge what you think is worth your skill and time. Money is no obstacle."

She told them she had to return to her with the cost. Both people left her with the mummy and drove off.

In an hour, Jan would come around with fresh plants. What would he say about the mummy?

Shop is Sold

A week later, the shop was sold. When a couple came in, asking her if she wanted to sell the shop, she responded immediately.

She was amazed at how fast their reality was changing from one day to the next, how everything just happened.

"How do you know the shop is for sale?" she asked because she had contacted an estate agent the day before, who was very unsure if she would get her money back.

"We saw in the newspaper that your house burned down and a few days ago, we heard that this is your shop. We just wondered. We are looking for an already established business we can buy."

"Well, all I want is to pay the bank the loan I took two years ago to start this shop."

"How much?"

"Ten thousand Rand."

The man stepped forward and shook out his hand. "Sold!"

His wife was smiling, waiting to congratulate him. She had been so stunned; she got what she wanted and asked for without any agent fees.

"Let's draw out a contract, and when we are both happy, I will pay you the money; the shop is ours."

He had asked for a month for her to keep the shop running for them and for them to get their money ready. He would join his wife in running the shop after that. At the same time, they wanted to keep buying sand art arrangements from her for the shop.

She was even more amazed that she was already being offered an ongoing little income when the shop was sold. Telling Jan her news pleased her even more after he had been so negative

Their New Rented Home

How it all came together was still a miracle. The home that became vacant was on the same street they lived in. Only a few houses away.

The bank paid the rent while they kept paying the house loan, as always, when their home was being rebuilt.

Living in a rented house with hand-me-down furniture, bedding, and a picnic garden set was initially challenging, but they decided to build a new home on the same plot. They were all glad to be living away from that strange family they had nothing in common with but would always be grateful for their hospitality at a time of need.

The Egyptian Mummy

The mummy could not stay in the shop after it was officially sold. She had often seen tall, thick, empty cardboard drums Johan had stacked into his back garden. They were used to transport electric cables. On the way to their rented home, she went past Johan's house to ask him if she could use them to rest the mummy in the kitchen. After seeing the mummy in the back seat, he delivered them later.

The kids were mystified after she took many books on Egypt out of the library.

"How can I fix these cuts? I need to bandage it again but with what?" Jan was drinking coffee, sitting on a hand-me-down barstool in the kitchen.

"I know. Take the old tent the dogs are sleeping on, tear the strips as wide as the bandage, and use wood glue. That is at least organic."

She looked at him in absolute amazement. "Yes, and I will dye the green canvas first to grey. How clever of you."

The following weeks were taken up with making the leather mask by wet moulding leather over a fashion dummy she had bought from a scrapyard. Fixing the bandage at home and occasionally helping the new owners get familiar with the running of the shop. They visited regularly, and she could not wait to hand the shop over for good.

The weird but wealthy woman was pleased with her work and even commissioned her to make a coffin with leather images on it. Jan made one, and she covered it with leather. She earned a great deal of money from this job and never saw or heard from the woman ever again.

She purchased a second-hand Pfaff sewing machine to replace the one that had been burned.

Building a New House

The months that followed were a new learning curve. She had become an unofficial building manager on site. To see a house being built in South Africa was an eye-opener. More or less unskilled labour was asked to do jobs for which they were not trained.

She had not been to the building site yesterday, so she was keen to see how far they got. The short walk with the three dogs had become a regular exercise.

The workforce had also just arrived in an open-loaded small truck with bags of cement.

The Building Site.

In stunned silence, she looked at a tall single brick wall going up to a point where the second-storey roof would be resting. Surely, that could not be. One strong gust of wind would topple that over.

"Mac Iver, the foreman of the labour force, greeted her with his toothless smile.

"Something doesn't look right to me. Why did they brick a single huge double-story wall without any support? Look at the plan. There is supposed to be a window there."

"Oh, no problem; later, we will just cut out a hole in the window."

The chaps standing around all agreed.

"I do not think so, but I will get the builder on the phone."

After a short moment, the builder arrived. He also looked up in stunned silence.

He shook his head in dismay and instructed the man to break down the wall. He apologized to her for being away at another site.

"I was about to phone you. I knew that is not how a double story is built, but I cannot tell that to the guys."

"No, I understand. They were eager to finish the work instead of waiting for further instructions."

He was a nice enough guy, a civil engineer turned into a house builder, but how much did he know?

Christmas in their Double Story Home

Six months had gone by since the fire. It was December, and they were all happy to occupy their new double-story home before Christmas.

"Mom, how do we get up to the second floor?" Sonja looked doubtful at the tall drum Jan used to climb up. He was tall to understand the space under the steeply pitched roof.

"I told you both, we must build the staircase. It will be extra. The builder had already exceeded his budget, and they both agreed that having a double-story house back, including a main en-suite bathroom, a modern open-plan kitchen, new carpets, and tiles in the hallway, was more than they had bargained for.

"Come, let's pack both cars, and Lucas help Dad to carry the garden furniture and mattresses.

Living so close to their new home, they would save money by moving whatever they had already accumulated again. Jan had ordered the timber for the staircase, and she had made curtains for the windows in the front of the house.

Chapter Ten

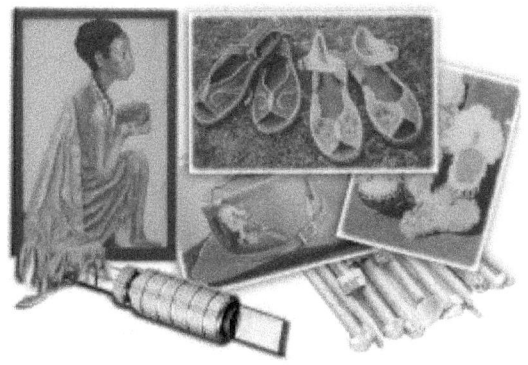

Their Brand New home

E very new day, walking around her new home was like a miracle. She had never truly liked her old home, no matter what Jan had done to it. Now it seems that what she truly wanted for a house had just materialized. Yes, they needed furniture and many other items. She remembered it was gone whenever she looked for a knife or any other simple household gadget. Even the light switches or kitchen drawers were in a different place.

The two months in their new home seemed like a lot longer. Jan had made the staircase, and he was busy upstairs closing the roof trusses for Sonja's future bedroom on his days off work.

The doorbell was also a different tune. She had invited her Yoga friends for morning coffee.

"Wow! I can't believe it. How did you..." There they were. Sophie, Cynthia and Mel. They came in one car.

"Hi, let me show you all around before having coffee."

"Did you have to pay in? Is your house bond increased?" Cynthia asked.

"No, that has stayed the same." she was proud to show them around their new home.

"Well, your fire seems almost a well-planned accident...sorry that I flipped that out, but you know what I mean." Sophie had always been outspoken, which was unusual for an English-speaking South African lady, but she loved her for it, so she had to laugh.

"You are not the first to make that suggestion, believe me."

They were all peeping at what the upstairs looked like. Jan had made a floor to walk on, but it was still primarily open by seeing the roof tiles and many supporting beams.

"My parents are arriving next week, so the kids need to share a bedroom for now unless Sonja can sleep upstairs."

"They must be so pleased for you after all the dramas."

"Yes, we are all very pleased with our new home. Sometimes I miss some of the stuff from the past, but we all learned it was just stuff."

"Yes, thank goodness for your animals. They survived."

Cynthia hit the nail on the head. The thought of losing the dogs or even the budgie through fire would have been far more traumatising.

Survival Camp

Lucas came home from scouts telling them he wanted to join a Survival camp in Sedgefield for ten days during school holidays, five days of which they would spend alone in the woods. For this, he needed a medical bill of health.

"Seriously, how strenuous is this camp?"

"Some boys do not make it, but I will." Lucas, who had been a sickly boy until his last high-temperature scare when he was twelve, now looked as healthy as she had ever seen him. Her sixteen-year-old heart throb was determined. All she could think was how four years ago, they were anxiously waiting for the lab results that he might have leukaemia due to his abnormal blood cell counts. Thank goodness it came back negative.

"Good, let's have that medical test and tell the doctor why you need it."

Jan agreed. That test would prove to them that he now had a clean bill of health.

Lukas came back with an unsigned medical form. He had ingrown toenails that needed to be removed. Lucas had organised to have it done so he could join the camp two weeks later.

While he was away, the ten days were nerve-wracking, especially hearing from other parents that this camp was more challenging than army basic training.

Sedgefield

They were invited to visit the boys on the last day after a completion ceremony.

When they arrived, she spotted two boys with ligaments in plaster. There was no sign of Lucas.

"Gosh, Mom, where is he? Sonja uttered while peering at all the boys who were greeting their families.

They got out of the car and walked to the back of the building when they spotted him.

"Lucas, oh boy, you must have..."

"Hi, Moms, let's go home," Lucas remarked.

"How was it? Was it bad?" She hugged him as she could feel the bony knobs of his spine beneath his thin shirt. He had lost a lot of weight in 10 days.

Lucas did not share everything that had happened, but some of it was enough.

Family Visits

Her parents and sister were visiting with her nine-month-old baby girl in the coming week.

The airport was three minutes away by car, so they were excited to show off their new home. Sonja and Lucas had moved upstairs. They seemed to love it, but Jan had not yet made the rooms. Just all the ceilings and walls were done and painted. Her sister and her baby would sleep in the front bedroom while her parents were in what used to be Sonja's bedroom.

"My Mom and Dad will be so impressed." When she spotted them, she saw that her dad was old. He looked thin.

"Oh, you both are growing up so fast, and I heard you are now at College. Her Dad was tired from the flight.

Lucas was in matric and unsure what he wanted to do after that.

"Come let me show you your bedroom." They purchased a queen-size bed so they would be comfortable.

"It's in the same place as the other bedroom, but I love the built-in cupboards."

"Yes, the two bedrooms are the same size except ours. We now have a main-on suite taken from the original bedroom. Mom, what is wrong with Dad?"

Her mom was looking so sad; she braced herself for the worst.

"Dad will have an operation when we get back. It's colon cancer, and they are taking most of it out and replacing it with a stoma. He wanted to see you all before the ..." her mom couldn't say more.

Road Trip for Two Sisters

Both her parents suggested while they were looking after Annemarie's nine-month-old baby girl, they should take a breakaway and take a road trip together.

Her dad seemed to be fine and pottered about in the garage while her mom sat outside doing her word puzzles while the baby was asleep.

"You sure we will get to Cape Town in your car?"Annemarie looked very sceptical at the rust of her Volkswagen Passat and took some photos to show at home.

It was understandable for her to wonder about the safety of her old car because her lifestyle was so different. Annemarie was used to new luxury cars.

"Come, it's fine. We will leave early tomorrow before the kids are off to school, and Mom will take care of Carina."

Annemarie seemed very relaxed to leave her little girl with her parents since they had looked after her often in Holland. She was genuinely looking forward to getting to know her sister again. She would pay for the petrol and drive the car while Annemarie would pay for all the other expenses during their trip. She had already marked several stopovers on the map before arriving at Cape Town. They planned to be away for around ten days.

Plettenberg Bay.

Her first stop for lunch was just after storms River Bridge.

"Gosh, it is beautiful here. Let's sit outside and order something to eat at the restaurant overlooking the ravine below."

The weather was sunny and warm with a slight breeze. She was glad to stretch her legs. They had been driving for two and a half hours.

"After lunch, we will stop at the Big Tree, my favourite spot in Tsitsikamma forest. We have to walk in the garden of Eden." she was truly in her element. She was showing off the beauty of this part of the world where they lived. This is not like Holland, where there were no prehistoric forests. If only she would one day live in a place like this.

"Oh look, monkeys!"

"Monkeys and baboons roam wild here, but they love begging for food." She warned her sister not to feed them.

More cars were parked on the side of the road, and several monkeys were gathering closer.

The warm weather and being together with her sister around this part of the world was such a wonderful experience; she never wanted it to end.

"Let's drive further; I want to walk to the Big Tree in the forest." They were both wearing sunny dresses and sandals, looking smart but casual.

She drove into the parking bay when she saw the sign pointing to the right. It was still not too crowded, being early on a weekday.

The Big Tree

The sign on the side of the road told them that the Outeniqua Yellowwood Tree is around 1,000 years old.

To walk in a prehistoric forest took her away from all the relationship frictions at home. On the way, during their two-hour drive, her sister shared some of her disappointments with finding out about her husband having a child by someone who used to be his secretary.

Walking amongst tree ferns and many other smaller tropical plants and moss was like being in a magic landscape. After a while, the winding path took them to her favourite spot.

"Gosh, this tree is tall." The sign said that had an impressive height of 36.6 meters.

They took turns standing against the trunk of the big tree, touching her while taking photos with Annemarie's fancy camera. As she felt the energy coming from this giant, wondering what stories these three could share if only by touching it, she speculated that it might be downloaded into her mind. More and more people arrived, so they walked back to her car.

There were no monkeys to be seen, and for that, she was grateful.

Storms River Mouth

The next stop would be towards the ocean on the left. They drove to Storm's river mouth so she could show Annemarie a fantastic suspension bridge.

"Can we walk on it?" They were both not dressed for hiking.

"Yes, that is the idea." We have to look for accommodation when we arrive in Plettenberg Bay later. Is that OK?"

It was a real treat for her to sleep over in accommodation she could not have paid for. Money was tight. They were still battling to purchase things they had lost in the fire.

Annemarie was having a ball. She took many photos. They stayed over in a brilliant hotel, and after a full breakfast, Annemarie took more pictures of the luxurious houses on the hill overlooking the ocean. She imagined living in this part of the world as heaven.

The little gift shops and clothing boutiques catering to tourists were for her to get ideas for her leatherwork. She needed to find out how to supply her handcrafted bags to these shops.

Knysna.

Annemarie was in her element after lunch and shopping for presents in the many shops.

"Imagine having a holiday house here.

"Yes, I'm sure many people from Johannesburg and overseas do. During the off-season period, the locals have a hard time. They make most of their money during the December and Easter holidays."

During one of her yoga get-togethers on Wednesdays, she learned about family members farming in the Knysna area.

The Wilderness

After stopping at the Knysna heads for a drink, the afternoon was getting on, and she wanted to stop at the wilderness where a famous leather artist, Beatrice Bosh lives. She loved her leather art and was inspired to create leather wall hangings herself from the clothing scraps that had started to sell at Art-in-the-Park every month.

Oudtshoorn

After staying near Oudtshoorn, they booked a tour to the Cango Caves.

"Gee Hendrika, I'm not going any deeper. It's too scary, and I cannot take my camera."

She looked down at the iron stepladder and into a deeper part of the cave, but some people were not allowed to go further due to it being too big. ...more like this, he said. The guide showed some photos of very overweight people. He was very polite.

"I'm keen. See you just now." Crawling through the caves was so narrow that people with claustrophobia would not manage, primarily through the chimney and the letterbox. Annemarie was filming her when she came out on the other side. She was exhausted.

Gordon's Bay

The following day, the drive from Oudtshoorn to Gordon's bay took over six hours.

Annemarie's husband had family living in Gordon's Bay, and when they heard she was visiting her family in Port Elizabeth, she got an open invitation.

"Do you know them?" she asked when they got closer nearer when the road sign said Hermanus.

"No, not really. I think Tom's nephew remarried an Afrikaans woman, and that is all I know." They were following a map, but she had no idea that Gordon's Bay was sixty kilometres from Cape Town.

"Let's ask for directions before it gets dark". She was genuinely stiff from her crawl in the Cango Caves. Her lower back was complaining from being sitting behind the wheel.

They arrived at Strand, and the address was not far, and it was higher, according to the directions.

Annemarie's English was not all that fluent, and she wouldn't drive on the left side of the road, but she knew that before they went on the trip. So far, they had a great time together.

It was already dark when they found the address. They were on the lookout and had snacks and drinks ready.

Vineyards and Apple Orchards

Their host was a super guy and drove them around many places. Seeing how the apples were packed for export and wine tasting was a luxurious experience. Annemarie didn't drink wine at all but pretended to like it. They served all kinds of cheeses and did not have to pay for them. What a treat.

The following day, their host took them to some very expensive houses for which he was an agent. She had never seen Jewish homes that had more than one kitchen. All on different levels. One home had an incredibly steep one-way driveway into a double garage, and with a remote control, they parked on a turntable platform that took the car at a 90-degree angle to drive out again.

"These houses must cost a lot of money." Thinking at their brand new home that had replaced their thirty thousand rand home.

"Oh yes, in the millions."

His Afrikaans wife was somewhat strange. She never joined them, but they were glad to move on the way home the following morning.

Chapter Eleven

Port Elizabeth.

They took two days to travel home, and when they arrived in the early evening, her mom and dad were happy to see them, so were Sonja and Lucas

"We do have something to show you?" Her mom said with a mysterious look while Annemarie took a peep into her bedroom, where Carina was fast asleep. She phoned home from her cell phone, talking to the two other children who were missing their mommy. It was a costly phone call, but Tom was a successful businessman who could afford it.

We were both trying to guess what was so secret, and her mom wanted to tell, but dad stepped in, saying to wait for the next day. They all wanted to know about the trip. Jan had cooked dinner, and Sonja laid the dinner table. They had waited for us to eat together.

The following day, Annemarie knew the secret. Carina had started to walk. She was sad to have missed it, but to see her tiny baby girl already taking free steps was in itself a miracle, for she had been in an incubator for being born far too early.

Leatherwork Changes

Ever since after the fire and designing Sonja's matric dance dress that included white soft clothing leather as a feature, the direction of her leatherwork started to shift. She would still design bags and other fashion or decor items, but her challenge to design leather jackets for the whole family took priority. Having lost all their clothing in the fire and not having a shop to look after, she wanted to be self-employed again, but in a different direction..

Sonja had chosen to enter college in Port Elizabeth, where they offered a course on becoming a buyer. She knew Sonja had an academic mind and could easily have entered university with her high school marks, but the cost was horrendous.

Jan refused to borrow a study loan to become an optician since she was impressed with wearing contact lenses. Sonja was also keen to become a fashion entrepreneur.

Teaching Sonja to Drive

Entering college meant Sonja needed to get her driving license. In the beginning, she drove her to the PE University, but her lecture hours were so irregular that for her to get there herself was the best solution.

She had already taken her for driving lessons in her Passat at the shopping parking lot, but the plan was to pay for a few proper lessons from the driving school.

They still had the station wagon, but Jan was now driving a company car, so three motor vehicles were parked in the driveway.

"Why is the station wagon parked funny at the front?" she asked as she walked through the front door. She had come back from her afternoon leather classes at the Art college while both Sonja and Lucas were home.

"Lucas needed something from the shop, so I took him."

"What, Moppie? Is that so? "

"Mom, I never went onto the main road, but don't tell Dad."

"That's it. You need to get your license. I hope you are ready to take your written exam so we can go to a driving school with those papers.

They started to look in the papers for a second-hand car for Sonja

Starting a Leather Jacket Adventure

Jan, Lucas, and Sonja were the first to wear her leather jackets, and Piet from Johannesburg ordered one for himself later.

Her jacket designs were often named after the person she had designed them for, and slowly, she started to use Sonja's bedroom downstairs, where her parents had stayed, as her sewing room.

Through her prickly pear gift shop, which she had before the fire, she had befriended several Dutch friends who were all shocked to hear about their home that had gone up in smoke. The one family owned a Protea farm outside PE. They delivered export bunches to her shop that were not good enough for the export market. The wife from the UK loved knitting, and when she saw the clothing out of leather, they made a deal to share their skills. She would knit a unique creative top with several different textured types of wool that she would exchange for a leather skirt.

Her other Dutch friend Ellie and her husband, a builder, became good friends, more to her than to Jan. Ellie loved leather clothing, so she started to design a jacket for her. They were slowly getting on their feet, running a takeaway place nearby, but they were hiring a car.

After speaking to Jan, they decided to give them their fully paid station wagon as long as they had organised the papers. The generosity overwhelmed them, and she felt suitable for giving them a car to get around in. Having a vehicle standing idle and not being used when they were paying to hire transport was not correct.

Sonja's Self-Employed Adventure

They purchased a refurbished red Beetle for Sonja, who would pay them back in instalments when she began to earn.

Sonja and two friends from college wanted to start a clothing boutique. Two of the other mothers would sew, so Sonja suggested that she could design a smart casual tracksuit line. Three girls rented a market stall inside the building for a start, and she would pay part of the rent that gave her space for two clothing racks.

"You are sure that will take off?"

"Mom, I would love to earn my own money while working for myself. Waitressing is not for me. I looked at some very smart tracksuits, let me show you. I've cut out some images from magazines."

The idea inspired her. Who knows if one idea would sell, she might look out for a part-time seamstress to help her. All she needed was the capital for the material. She would see if she could sell some outfits wholesale to Sonja and have to work out what markup it could take.

She started with two different styles of tracksuits in three sizes: small, medium and large. Combining various textures and some leather trimming resulted in a brilliant outfit.

In between her leatherwork for her outlet at Art in the Park one Sunday in the month, her sewing room in the house was slowly getting too small.

"Mom, I made my first sale". It was music to her ears when Sonja came home from her afternoon part-time shift at the boutique in between college classes.

"Tell me which one." They had been open for two days, so that was a good start. Sonja shared her time as a saleslady with two girls.

Each had different clothing line designs. Hers would always have a leather trimming as a kind of brand mark.

Being an Entrepreneur

Lucas played rugby as a required sport, but she hated the idea. The injuries some boys came home with made her question the game's safety. After two seasons, he lost interest and instead enrolled for the St Johns ambulance training after hours when he was still in matric. He would attend all the sports events as a medic.

Jan was often home late from work, so they had dinner together, and she kept some for him in the oven.

They started to live very separate lives. She was more involved with her small business and combined it with proving to the kids that being an entrepreneur was not such a bad thing.

Holding on to a job you did not like was not necessarily in her mind. Her income was irregular, and she could not yet support a family as Jan did. For that, she was grateful for having the opportunity to make a start, but she was never getting talked into getting a regular job.

Her unhappiness in her marriage was often suppressed by keeping busy. She knew she yearned for some approval from Jan, but that was never forthcoming.

Buying up Clothing Leather Scraps.

She had discovered that she could buy large leather offcuts in bags from a big clothing factory. Gradually, she sorted the larger pieces and decided to design leather jackets with them. In the evenings, she started to make leather jewellery from the smaller scraps, earning extra pocket money to put back into her cottage industry business.

Jan still mentioned her getting a real job, but she was having far too much fun growing her small leather gift and clothing business. In between, she had made a large leather sliding door for their new home after it had been displayed at the environmental display in town.

Sonja's Boutique

"Mom, one of the girls, has found shop premises on an excellent street."

"Then the rental will be high. Is that wise?"

"Well, we are selling, but we would have a far better passing trade, and one more girl would be joining us. One of the mothers is prepared to sign the lease. We could add some leather jackets. That will fetch a lot more money.

Lucas Turns Eighteen.

When he turned eighteen, Lucas got a job as a barman at the yacht club to earn some pocket money.

Her days were full of many activities. Two days a week to aerobic, then housework and sewing for Sonja's clothing rack in the part of the shop she paid rent for. She was in her second year at college when she met her first boyfriend.

Sonja's Boyfriend

Sonja's boyfriend, Tim. a good-looking keen surfer, was two years older than Sonja and studied graphic design. He was very besotted with Sonja and became a regular visitor after lectures and between his surfing. Seeing his surfboard and sometimes surfer friends who were also visiting became a regular scene.

Tim was looking for part-time earnings, so she got him involved in airbrushing material for discotheque skirts and tops that became a real hit with teenagers.

He was driving an ancient car that looked as if it was held together by duct tape compared to Sonja's red beetle, which she was paying off with her earnings.

Lucas had still no idea what he wanted to study. And she was worried that he would be called up for the army after his matric exam. A war was going on at the Angola border, and many South

African soldiers were sent there. In no way did she feel patriotic enough to see Lucas ending up there, so she was determined to get him into college instead.

Jan followed her suggestions and supported her effort to inspire Lucas to study something, even if it was something he might change later.

His army call-up papers had arrived. She was in an uproar.

"But Mom, I do not mind; I'll go.

"No way. I would rather send you to Holland to your grandparents and Annemarie."

"But I want to go into the army.

"Then go when you have a college degree of some sort. Then, at least you end up enlisting at a higher rank." it took all the persuasions to get him signing up for a civil engineering drafting diploma course."

Lucas was not happy about his parent's suggestions. Still, knowing that Sonja's boyfriend said he was going to Pretoria after finishing his studies, he signed up for a civil engineering course.

Becoming an Employer

Her first employee was Anna, a German woman in her sixties who had first reacted to her ad and worked two days a week. She was looking for a part-time income to add to her German pension.

The bedroom that used to be Lucas' bedroom was now also turned into a sewing room. Lucas's bedroom was now upstairs. She had employed another girl, Lia, to help her make clothes and leather jackets for Sonja's shop. The business was growing.

"Hendrika, there is a woman to see you. She is a haberdashery sales rep." Lia called her from the back room. She was cutting leather for several leather jackets she had designed herself. The front room was purely for sewing.

Lia, a twenty-seven-year-old petite girl with very thick, dark, tight, curly hair, was now her full-time assistant who took her work seriously. She had contacted her from a newspaper advert a month after Anna.

"Ok, thanks, let's see what she has for sale. Please take her to the lounge."

"Oh, she is already in the showroom."

"Hi, I'm Justine, and I love what you are doing here. I'm sure you will love what I can show you in the line of arty buttons."

Justine was around her age, a tall, hefty-looking woman with dark curly hair, black-rimmed glasses, and a very open, bubbly personality. She made herself very comfortable and engaged them all in what she had to sell. She was still there when Lia went home, and Jan arrived home from work.

Jan laughed at her stories about how she became a sales rep. She liked a job where she was not stuck in an office and worked her hours.

Lucas had never shown any interest in sports, and driving him to college was a drag if his lecture hours did not coincide with his sister's, but there was no money for another car.

Their home was entire of young people most of the time, so Jan started to complain, but she loved it.

Finding the Act centre

Justine, the haberdashery sales rep, became a regular visitor and often stayed for dinner, making Jan and her wonder who was cooking at her home.

Justine had two children younger than hers. They had both just entered high school. She and her UK husband had lived in Rhodesia but had to leave after Prime Minister Ian Smith of white-ruled Rhodesia, whose attempts to resist black rule dragged the country into isolation and civil war. They had to go with very little.

"The books on your bookshelf remind me of the Act Centre," Justine remarked after telling her about Lobsang Rampa, an author who wrote paranormal and occult themes. Her little bookshelf was

full of new-age titles, and she kept it upstairs because Jan did not like
to see them.

"Oh, why?"

"They preach that kind of stuff or at least a Rhodesian friend told
me, but I've never been. Shall we go on a Sunday when they give a
service?"

"Oh, is it a church?"

"Not really, but people come together on a Sunday. I'm curious.
Let's go. I will pick you up on Sunday just before ten. I seem to
remember that they start at eleven.

Chapter Twelve

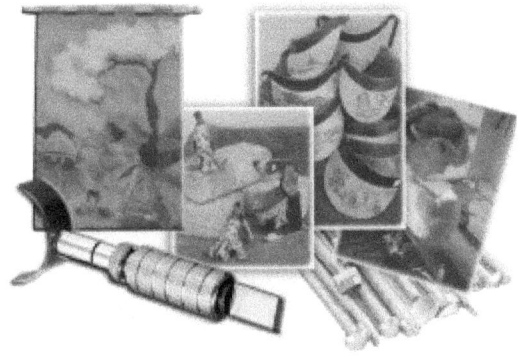

Like-Minded Individuals

W here are you going all dressed up on a Sunday morning?"

"Jan, I told you last evening. To a centre where they give Sunday morning talks about topics of an esoteric nature, or that is what Justine told me."

"That is devil's stuff." Jan's expression was as if he wanted to puke, but she knew by now that he was lashing out at her.

"How do you know? She also said it was more about the science of mind and how something works. Like a kind of philosophy. Why don't you join us?"

Her reflection in their bedroom mirror was as if she was dressed up for a church, and that was not her intent. The front doorbell was the break she needed. Jan's reaction towards her always hit her into her solar plexus.

"Mom, when will you be back?" Sonja's boyfriend Tim had also arrived with his surfboard tied on the roof without a roof rack.

"Hi there, are you both going out, looking all dressed smartly?" Tim replied, looking at the two women, Justine and herself. He was a real charmer.

Lucas came down the stairs, clearly smelling the fried bacon and eggs. Justine looked like she would love to join Jan, and he knew it. The hallway started to get crowded.

"No idea when Sonja. We don't know how long the service is; hopefully, it will not be like a church service, but we will find out. I see that you are off to the beach with Tim. Will you both be home for dinner?"

"Come, Tim, join us for breakfast and let these women go to their church or whatever they call the centre. "Jan interrupted from the kitchen, waving his hands to say go away.

"It's the ACT centre, not a church," she said."

"What does Act stand for?" Tim asked, playing the interested boyfriend.

"Association of Creative Thought" Justine replied. She never got a reply about dinner. A part of her wanted to spend time with them all for breakfast, but she was also keen to learn about this A.C.T centre.

Nature is our Greatest Teacher.

The first talk was so inspiring. The woman who was the speaker was about her age and a qualified marine biologist, and she showed everyone how nature is a silent teacher, friend, philosopher, and guide. Animatedly, she talked about how, metaphorically, small animals can remove all our pain, agonies, grief and despair.

"The only limits are those we place on ourselves, for there are no limits. If we merge with everything around us, we will be in an elevated state of consciousness.

She looked around her audience, and her silence was somehow very effective.

"There are no sides in our outlook on life except how we choose to experience it. Unfortunately, very few will go inside to resolve their discussion and debate about what and who they are, so they take a side other than their own."

Gosh, that was so very true! Jan took a very different approach to life.

"Nature shows all her wealth irrespective of who we are and what we are. It never distinguishes between good and evil but rather removes all the negativities. It fills us with all positive energy.

The lecturer was looking at her notes and carried on.

"Have you ever realized how our brains resemble clouds? In a sense, our thoughts come and go as the clouds move in the sky.

"Have you paid attention to the flower? The fragrance of a flower is formless. There is always room for the sun to come and shine. The petals do not create obstacles for each other; they create room for the sun."

This sermon was nothing like what preachers preach from the culprit. She was engrossed in the concepts the speaker shared.

"The study of metaphysics and the laws of mind leads to an enfoldment in consciousness."

That was so for her. Looking around, I saw that everyone looked normal, not hippies or new-age people. After the talk, tea and coffee were offered in the other room, where many books for sale were on display.

A woman who knew Justine greeted them both. She was introduced, and simultaneously, the woman who had given the talk joined them.

"Why don't you join my Divine Science evening classes?" she asked them. That was after she had complimented her and felt like she had come home to a like-minded community.

They both signed up for evening classes on awakening their inner potential as spiritual beings. To have found a meeting place where individuals seek a deeper purpose in life was just up her street.

Expanding Her Cottage Industry

Her leatherwork had by now turned into a leather clothing business. Having two people working from their homes during the day was restricting, but the daily sales from Sonja's combined boutique were so encouraging. Designing leather clothes was a daily challenge.

Jan was often home after they all left around five, but he never remembered which evening they would eat dinner early.

"I told you the workshop classes are on a Thursday evening."

"You are getting increasingly involved with this A.C.T centre and their activities."

"Well, it's not as if we as a couple have an active social life in the evenings?" Jan was pouring a glass of wine for them both in the kitchen while she was ready to dish supper in the dining room. She was reluctant to decline, knowing it might not be appropriate for her workshop evenings.

"Tomorrow evening, I have a lifeline shift."

"I will probably not be home. There is a ship in, and I might stay on until it's finished."

"Lucas, Sonja, come to have dinner," she called from below the staircase. They were both in their bedrooms upstairs.

Their three spaniels were running down at her mentioning dinner. Snoopy was getting old, and she noticed her lump getting bigger.

"Mom, what is wrong with Scamper?"

He was also under medication after he had been run over early last year. He had suffered internal injuries to do with his bladder. Sonja was always the first to spot any trouble.

"Why?"

"He is smelling like piss again; let's get him outside and see if he will do a wee." Lucas took them all out while dishing up their supper. As always, Snoopy was the most greedy of the three, but she growled at the young spaniel puppy. He was left over from last year's litter, but it was too much for Snoopy.

Jan got his second glass of wine, or was it his third?

"Why you don't stay home this evening, he said with a slur.

"Come, let's eat. Justine is coming to fetch me just now," ignoring him. She hated it when he started to drink more than he should.

"Tim is picking me up; we are going to see a movie," Sonja announced. Lucas wanted to know what movie. She was still grateful to have both kids around the dinner table, but it was getting rarer. Each had functions, activities, or, in Jan's case, his work, which took him away.

"Let's organise a barbeque this weekend." Jan nodded. He loved having people over for a braai, so he must be accessible. She suggested it out of guilt for going out tonight and tomorrow evening for LifeLine.

Her spaniel puppy was asking for attention. She fed him some of his favourite snacks.

"Sonja", she turned to her as she prepared to leave. "Ask Tim if his parents would like to come. I'll ask Justine, her husband, and her Dutch friends to whom Justine introduced us two weeks ago at her house.

"The carpenter?" Jan had been talking to him more than she did. The food must have settled the alcohol in his stomach because his voice stopped slurring.

"No idea what he does for a living? His wife works for a kitchen building place in Newton Park."

"That is near where the Prickly Pear used to be," Sonja replied when the front bell rang. Both Justine and Tim had arrived.

The Science of Mind Classes

There were ten people in the evening class. Some she had already met at that Sunday service. One was the friend Justine knew from Rhodesia. There were several couples who all seemed to have been Justine's friends when they lived in Salisbury.

She had heard horror stories from Tim's parents at a birthday party a few weeks ago at Justine's house. They all had to flee more or less with practically nothing. Leaving their home with whatever they could fit into their car.

"Has anyone of you done any reading homework?" Valery, the Sunday lecturer, a tall, hefty, muscular-looking woman with short white curly hair, asked.

She also loved the comments of Ingrid and Tom, a retired couple who attended the class. She was very drawn to Ingrid and often wished she could ask her questions instead of Valery. Somehow, she knew that Ingrid was very wise and aware. So was her husband, but less so. She planned to chat with her during their break.

She was still battling with some concepts they had to study at home, but she kept that to herself.

Sometimes, Lucas would join her on a Wednesday evening for a half-hour meditation at the Act Centre, but she tried not to talk too much about her already alternative viewpoints, just in case he would be put off by it like his dad was.

Doing the Evening Shift at LifeLine

She arrived at the Lifeline flat to take over from Cynthia, who had done the shift before her. She had not seen her for some time. Ever since they moved to Walmer and with her clothing business, there was hardly any time for Yoga. She went instead to aerobic classes nearer by.

"Hi there, how are you? Have not seen you in ages." they hugged, and Cynthia told her that ever since her son and Sophie moved to their smallholding outside PE, Sophie stopped coming to Yoga, so instead, she took on more Lifeline duties.

"It's getting increasingly difficult for me to do lifeline duties during the day, and Jan complains about me going out in the evenings."

"Is he still so against you being interested in alternative philosophies?" Cynthia knew about her marriage problems.

"Oh, he has not changed. I'm learning that I cannot change people; they must want to change themselves. Any special calls I should know about?"

It's been very quiet, with only two regulars. You can read up on them in our report book.

When she settled in to read the reports from a few days before, she recognised some callers. Some were creepy, wanting to shock more than anything else. They had been trained to recognise the callers who just wanted to chat because they were lonely. Closing a call was not easy, but they had to do it just in case there was another caller who was suicidal.

She was always nervous when a call came in. Lifeline had only one phone line and was alone in the flat.

Her usual: "This is Lifeline. Can I help you." was followed by a long silence.

"Are you there?" she asked. Then, the caller hung up. She wrote it in the report book while waiting for the next caller.

"Lifeline, can I..." Heavy breathing was followed by: "I hate my life....more breathing, which reminded her of her friend Pat, who died from lung cancer, but this was a man's voice. "Is breathing difficult for you?" she said, in case she was wrong.

"Why?"

"Oh, dear, one of those men who want to ask questions instead of responding to her question.

"Some people have difficulty breathing; that's why I asked." He sounded like a man who might be acting out.

"You have an accent; where are you from?" Oh dear, another question.

"I'm Dutch. Do you mind telling me your name?" she waited.

"What is yours?" No breathing sounds, so here is someone who is maybe bored or what? She decided to stay silent to see if you would start talking.

"You can call me John, and I want my life to be over," she kept silent and replied, "I can hear that you are unhappy."

"I'm fed up. Life is not fear. My wife left me. My kids are grown up and have gone far away, and yes, I do have a problem breathing." he started coughing.

"John, I feel that having wishes might help you," she said, trying to steer him into a more positive mindset.

"Oh, I have many of those, but what is their use?" She could not suggest things, so her reply must put the ball in his court.

"I used to have expectations, but no one listened to me."

"I'm listening." he kept silent, and she heard someone talking in the background. So he was not alone. Then he hung up.

There were no calls for the rest of the evening. Instead, she read the report book and wondered if she should leave her volunteer work. Maybe her few years of Lifeline duties had come to an end. She would much rather get more involved with activities related to the Act Centre. She could not do both.

Visit the Local Tannery

Lately, she needed larger full leather skins for her designs, so a trip to the tannery just outside Port Elizabeth was the best option. Sonja told her that the girls were planning a fashion show in the community hall and that they had asked if I could design something special in leather.

She had some ideas and would call it wearable art in leather. In the meantime, they were making more and more items like bags with scrap leather pieces, and after her workforce had all gone home, she started to get ideas for wall hangings with the minor pieces. Her outside workroom was lately used more by Sonja's boyfriend Tim, who found a creative way to airbrush some of the materials after her sewing staff of by now five people had sewed them into party skirts and tops to match. They were a bestseller in Sonja's shop. He earned some pocket money that way from the airbrush work.

Designing clothes for Sonja's clothing boutique came easy for her. Especially when she had free rein to do what she liked, she loved creating waistcoats by combining leather with Dutch curtain lace and upholstery material.

She needed to think of expanding her outlets besides Sonja's shop because Sonja would not forever be involved with the girls running her side of the boutique that she learned after the fashion show.

She needed to think of ways to become more professional, and that was done by creating a catalogue of her upcoming season designs. With those, she hoped to attract Cape Town and Johannesburg sales agents.

Sonja was used as a model for her fashion line, which also included bags and leather jewellery.

She made many of these leather jewellery pieces during the evenings in the lounge on her low table on wheels Jan had made for her. Watching TV felt like a waste of time, so she combined it with doing most of the leather glueing work at night.

Flower Displays at the ACT centre.

The ACT centre had gradually become a haven for her on Sunday mornings and two evenings in the week. She became increasingly involved with the fundraising activities by decorating the hall for a dinner and dance event or when the Sunday school children presented a play they had been practising for weeks. She loved doing this, but it involved more and more time over weekends. She often tried to get Jan involved, but sadly, he was just not interested in meeting the people she had become friends with unless she invited them to their home for a barbeque.

Having met both Ingrid and Tom, the retired couple at home, she would get him to join her when a fundraising event included dinner and dance. Still, because he often tried to debate the philosophical topics of the members of the A.C.T. centre, she stopped getting him involved.

Gradually, she learned that she should not try to change him in any way, which she was still hoping for.

The lady who used to do the flower arraignments each Sunday morning at the service hall took ill, and she was approached after hearing that she used to own a flowering plant and gift shop. She still had all the flower contacts from which she could buy, so she could easily stay within the budget they allowed her each week. When the lady recovered, they shared the load arrangement.

Her Awakening Journey

Often, over the weeks and months that went by, Hendrika recalled that one profound experience: she heard a voice so many years ago when the children were still in primary school. At the time, she thought it was a warning about her smoking habits; ever since she had joined the A.C.T centre, more and more visions from that uncanny moment started to filter into her mind.

She started to understand how the law of attraction worked, but how to create or see a manifestation happening was another story.

Often, during or after meditations with Tom and Ingrid at their home, when she knew Jan was at work and Sonja and Lucas were out, she asked for guidance, but that voice never came until one moment while she was making coffee for the whole crowd at home after dinner.

Winning R1000 at Bingo Night

Sonja, Tim, Lucas, a new girlfriend, and Jan had all finished dinner, but none had made plans for the evening when the front doorbell rang. It was her friend, Justine, who was always around dinner time!

"Hi there, I'm so glad to catch you all; I need to sell the last Bingo tickets for the Lions Club. They are drawing the prize of a thousand rand tonight, and you are all invited."

As she made Justine's mug of coffee, she heard it.

"Prove it to them?"

She instantly knew what she was supposed to prove to them all. Knowing that she had picked up on a telepathic instruction, that moment while stirring coffees, her skin broke out in goose flesh.

"I will buy one ticket, Justine, and I will prove to you all that I will win the thousand rands by pure intent." Hearing herself saying that did trigger feelings of doubt.

"Oh really? How are you doing that?" Jan's voice challenged her.

"Like I said before, but I never knew if I could prove that we can all attract anything in life with our minds."

"Your mom is right; we learned that at the evening workshop. Come on, all of you, see if your mom can prove it."

"I tell you what. I will share my thousand rands with anyone who joins Justine and me for this Bingo evening." In the meantime, her heart was pumping from pure dare because she was taking a massive leap of faith.

"Dream it, feel it, taste it and see it happening."

That did it. They were all buying the last of the tickets in the booklet and decided to come along, which was a miracle.

"I'm going home to tell my kids what you said. I want them to experience that you will win. Is that OK?" Was Justine fully confident in her, or was she just as doubtful?

"Fine, tell them they also earn some money by joining."

Telling them that only her ticket would win the big prize, but nothing could stop them from aiming at other prizes, made her feel like she would jump off a cliff.

Knowing that her mental energy had to overpower all the thought energies from everyone at the Bingo evening to achieve what she promised would happen made her focus on what the feelings would be like winning, what a thousand rand in notes would look like, smell like and hearing her number being called.

During the drive to the Lion's Club Hall, she kept her mind clear of distractions from others. That itself was quite a mission. She was not listening to anyone but instead focused on winning the thousand rands.

They were all ten of them seated in a circle. All of them except Justine's children were wearing her leather jacket designs, which made some comments like," Those people do not need to win the thousand rands". Yes, they all looked very abundant, so she kept up, seeing her number be the last in the drum

While the draw was going on, she mentally focused on feeling delighted at winning the thousand rands after hearing her one-ticket number being the last called out.

When the last draw arrived, all she mentally saw was her ticket number.

YES, she won! She walked up to the podium, and her elation at achieving the wine and proving that her mind could manifest the winning number was more substantial than the money she walked away with. She was left with ninety rands by the time it was shared among them. What an evening.

Jan Changed Jobs Again

The rift between Jan and herself was getting larger and larger. It saddened her that it was so, but talking about it always resulted in the same argument. It was all her fault. Both children must know that their parents' relationship was not all that harmonious, but they kept it well hidden from the outside world.

"I've applied for an opening at the manganese ore terminal again," Jan mentioned before he got ready for work. It was still early, around seven O'clock.

"Really?" The Port Elizabeth port, which used to ship manganese ore from South African producers where Jan worked before, brought up many memories. Jan liked working there because of the free time in between ships.

"How come? Is there an opening?"

"There is. The one person you know, Nick, is moving to Richard Bay.

"Oh really? They never told us. We were there for a barbeque two weeks ago?'

"They asked him to run the brand new terminal in Richard Bay."

She was not surprised. Nick was a go-getter, not like Jan, who would never do more than what was required of him. She knew that Jan didn't take to Nick because of being ambitious, which Jan was not. He worked with him just before he was laid off due to budget cuts. So she thought, she never knew why.

She liked Nick and his wife Ria. They were about ten years older and lived about a thirty-minute drive away.

She would have loved living in Richards Bay, about one hour from Durban. A Tropical climate with lots of monkeys is all she remembered from their one-night camping trip years ago. That was after the official opening of the first phase of the harbour, which had been constructed for coal export.

She hoped that, for Jan's sake, he would get his old job back. At least he knew all about the work, but she was sure his hours would not be like it was before.

The little book by Richard Bach, Illusions, which she had bought at the Act Centre, was uplifting. It was a fantastic story about an unusual pilot. She was struck by the following:

"The bond that links your true family is not one of blood but of respect and joy in each other's life."

That rang true to her thinking about the people at the Act Centre, especially in the evening science of mind classes. It was as if the people there were part of a soul family she belonged to. Jan was not, but what about Sonja and Lucas?

Gosh, it's already eight O'clock. Soon her staff would arrive! Lucas and Sonja were already busy in the kitchen.

She had resigned from teaching at the art college and counselling for Lifeline long ago, but running a small cottage industry from home was also taking its toll.

Running a Business From Home

Her decision to change her work hours so that she was free after two O'clock in the afternoon was appreciated by her staff, especially since it did not affect their earnings. To have the house to herself after 2 o'clock was the best thing she could have done. When Jan came home earlier, there was also a good chance of finding the house empty of strangers.

They started one hour earlier and only took a half-hour break. Sonja was also happy when she came home from the shop and did not hear any sewing machines.

Her private time with her kids was special; she hoped everybody was running late.

Tim is Called up to the Army

"Mom, how can I ever find a buying job I like? Instead, I could apply for this post; what do you think?"

Reading the paper during breakfast was a regular activity these days. Sonja missed Tim, and soon, she would do her final exam. Sonja's Tim had been called up for the army straight after college, so he left for Pretoria.

"They were looking for someone who was good with figures and was willing to be trained for the stock market. Is that what you want to do?"

"There is nothing else going. I have been to the Edgars head office in Johannesburg to apply for a position as a trainee buyer, but they were not optimistic.

Sonja Finished College

Sonja's last days at college had arrived so fast that between keeping her business going, managing her sewing ladies and paying the salaries, buying leather and materials, bookkeeping and keeping in contact with the two clothing agents, little time was left for relaxing. Lucas was still working as a barman at the sailing club after college hours three times a week

Sonja got the job, which initially involved training about the stock market, but her heart was not in it.

Sonja had also applied for a job at Edgars, a large clothing store chain in South Africa, but heard nothing. She knew that she wanted to move to Johannesburg to be near Tim.

Jan got his old job back, but in between the ore shift, he was expected to help as an ordinary stevedore. His hours were more or less regular, and he got a company car again.

Johannesburg

After three months, Sonja got a letter from Edgars to come for an interview at their Edgars head office in Johannesburg.

"See, what you truly want might be around the corner."

"Yes, mom, wait and see. What do I tell my boss? That I'm flying to Johannesburg for just an interview, I might not get it."

"Oh, I know you will. Your heart is not into the stock change job, so take a few days off."

She already knew Sonja would soon leave home. It was a sad feeling, but at the same time, Sonja was ready to go home.

Flying to Holland to Say Goodbye

One evening, they were home by themselves. Jan cooked, and they shared a glass of wine.

"Jan, I think I want both children to see their grandfather for one more time while he is still alive."

"Oh, what makes you think he is dying?"

"My mom is worried. He is in a lot of pain and has lumps all over him. I'm sure the cancer came back. I have enough money for our air tickets. I will wait and see what happens with Sonja's interview. "

"Are you giving everybody off work?"

"Yes, I have to. They will have to understand."

"I hope so. I suppose you can say it's their holiday money earlier in the year."

Now that her mind was made up, she needed to wait for Sonja and find out when to book tickets for when Lucas had his college break.

The following day, Lucas came storming home from college, angry. He was doing his second term exams, and he had missed one due to his mistake of making a note of the exam day one day too late.

They were all upstairs, and the four ladies working for her were soon to go home when Lucas slammed his bedroom door shut.

She waited for everybody to leave work before speaking to Lucas, who was in his room sulking.

"What now? Do you have to do the whole semester all over again?" She asked, peeking around his bedroom door. Lucas was reading one of his favourite fantasy novels.

"No. I quit."

"What! Oh gosh, Lucas. Dad will be angry for having wasted the college fees. What do you suggest we tell him?" She was so disappointed it was hard not to show it.

"Mom, I have had another call-up, so I will go to the army in two weeks and see what I want to do after that."

"When did you get that? Oh no. I hate for you to get involved in fighting when it's not your country.

"I feel it is my country. I've been brought up here. I would not get a call up if it were not."

Her mind was spinning from the sudden changes. Lucas was in the Army, now that there was trouble at the Angola border. Was there honestly nothing she could do?

"I have to fetch your sister from the airport. Dad will come home late tonight, so let's get some takeaway. I do not feel like cooking tonight."

"Ok, I will join you. Moms do not worry. I will be okay." giving her a big hug.

Sonja had a big smile on her face when she walked towards them. She looked the part, smartly dressed with just a tiny business suitcase. She was so proud of her.

"Tell us. It's yes, you got a buyers job?"

Yes. It's a trainee buyer's job, but I start in six weeks. That gives me enough time to give my notice and ask Aunty Hilly if I can stay with her until I have found something to rent.

Hilly was Jan's younger sister, who worked as a ground flight attendant at the Johannesburg airport. "What are we getting for dinner? Kentucky or Pizza?" They both chose chicken and chips, which was easy. She could keep some for Jan when he came home late.

The kids ordered the food while she stayed in the car.

"I have something to tell you both when we are at home.

Chapter Thirteen

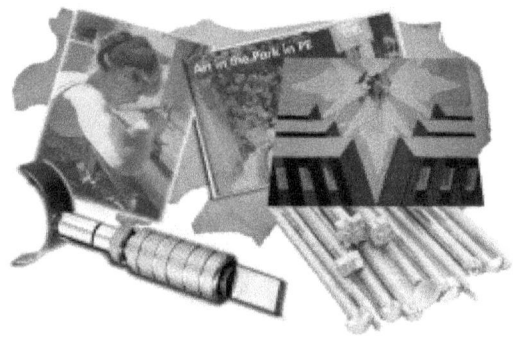

Children Are Leaving Home

"**M**om, what are you so secret about? Lucas already told me about him going into the army."

They gathered around the kitchen counter after she had finished feeding the dogs and Sonja's elderly cat, Tinkle.

"Grandpa is dying." Both kids were silent, taking it all in.

"Mom, is he in the hospital?"

"No, he is still with Oma at the place for older people, but I want you both to see him one last time while he is still alive."

"You mean now?"

"Yes, Lucas, I want to book a ticket for you if you do not mind flying alone since you are now free to go before you are called up to the Army."

"Wow! Does Opa know about us flying to Holland, especially to see him?" Like his dad, Lucas never showed many emotions, but he cared.

"No, not really. You will be staying with Annemarie and Tom. They will collect you from Schiphol."

Not that her sister was aware of what she suddenly told them, but she had to move fast. She would have to phone Annemarie first.

"I can't leave yet. Unless I tell them at work tomorrow." Lucas was still working as a barman at the yacht club, and the army would call him up at any moment.

"That is why I'm now making these plans. I have no airline tickets because I also want to go, but I must give people ten days' leave."

"Wow, they will love that, I'm sure. And gosh, Mom, that is a lot of money."

Lately, the three of them would eat dinner together. Jan often seemed to work late.

"Oh really, does Dad know? Is he going as well?"

"No, Moppie, Dad stays here. It's not his dad, anyway. Let's think about it all. I will visit the travel agent tomorrow to see what is available."

After finishing dinner, they both offered to do the dishes. She had to smile at that. Not that there were any, eating only on three plates.

She decided to phone Annemarie when both kids were watching television in the lounge.

Hendrika told all four ladies who worked for her about her trip and why. They were all very understanding. Sonja and she had booked a return ticket for two weeks in three weeks. Just before leaving for the army, Lucas would be back by then.

Lucas Flies to Holland

It was nerve-racking to bring Lucas all on his own to the airport. He had just enough time to visit his family for ten days. She felt it a shame that they could not all three fly together.

"Make the most of your time there. I'm sure Annemarie and Tom will show you around. Take photos."

"Yes, mom."

Lucas was growing up. A good-looking guy with big blue eyes many a girl would die for. He was also very courteous for his age. Her sister would love him, she was sure. The last time she saw him, he was twelve or thirteen.

"Ask Annemarie if you can call us when you are there."

Lucas Returns from His Trip

For ten days, she had not heard a peep from Lucas. She tried phoning Annemarie, but there was no reply during the day, and Jan would object for her to call in the evening.

She and Jan were at the airport, seeing him walking towards the terminal from the window. Her heart skipped a beat when he stepped inside.

"Hi, Moms, Dad, I could have walked home. "

"That will be the day. I know it is not far, but we are glad to see you. "

Her son looked more self-assured than when he left; at least, she thought so. His hair was getting long, knowing that would be gone the moment the army got hold of him.

"Tell us, how was Opa?" They had the house to themselves, and Jan made coffee. Sonja was visiting a friend. Jan seems to have no ships in and was just as keen to hear how Lucas' trip turned out. Usually, Jan would be in the garden and come in when she called him for dinner.

"He seems fine, mom. His walking is somewhat slow, but it was nice to see him. Oma as well, but their home is so small."

"It's a retirement home."

Lucas was not a talker, so she had to ask questions; otherwise, she would hear very little.

"Did you see Opa and Oma in Almelo?" Jan asked.

"Yes, dad, I took the train and phoned them when I was in Almelo." She was impressed. All on his own, travelling in a strange country. "And Annemarie and the kids?"

"They have a huge home, a pool and a tennis court." Lucas seemed impressed, but his replies didn't tell her about how he had been visiting alone.

"I still wish we could have all three gone together," was her reply while she started to prepare what to eat for dinner.

"Yes, me too," Lucas replied as he played with the dogs, who were still excited and happy that he was home.

"Really?" That was enough for her to pick up that he had been somehow lonely. It truly saddened her, but Sonja could not get out of her month's notice period, and Lucas's being called up so soon was unavoidable. She hugged him before he left upstairs to unpack his suitcase.

"Mom, the camping shop in Newton Park asked me to work almost full-time until I returned, so I will go there tomorrow before I leave for the army."

Mother and Daughter Flying to Europe.

Looking forward to travelling with just Sonja might have been a pipe dream. She was, after all, just over her teenager's syndrome and could not be like a girlfriend.

They stayed at Annemarie's place because there was no room at her parent's nursing home ground floor flat. It was tiny. However, the wealthy lifestyle of her sister did seem to do something to Sonja. Her dissatisfaction with herself and having to stay within a budget seem to have got to her.

Having an Out of Body Experience

Her dad was in a lot of pain, she knew. His colon cancer had returned but was now travelling through his whole body through his lymph glands. If only she could astral travel. Sometimes, she knew she had experienced being outside her body before, but she would jump back when she knew it. Why, she never knew. She had read all about it; she wondered if that was the reason.

She wanted to be with the people who passed over when Pat had years ago, but somehow, she never got very far. She had a suspicion that it was because she was not sleeping on her own.

Her dad was happy to see them, and so was her mom. They took the train from Annemarie's place to be with them as often as possible. The last time her dad insisted on walking with her mom to the station, she knew it was the last time she would see him.

"Take care," He said as they stepped inside the train. Her mom was planning to visit Annemarie, but she knew it would be after they had gone. It was hard to stop her tears on the train journey back to Annemarie's place.

"Mom, are you ok."

"Yes, I will be OK. I know it was a goodbye for good. " her voice broke from grief, but seeing her Dad in pain was just as bad. Sonja took her hand, and they were silent during the train journey.

For two weeks while they were in Holland, she wanted to include popping over to the UK for two nights, staying in a cheap hotel in London, and planning to meet with Jenny and Marisa and show Sonja around London.

London Visit

On the Ferry, via Dover to London, she explained the antennary

"This hotel room might not be so glamorous, but seeing London and meeting up with Jenny is nice. Not so?"

"I suppose so."

"Let's go and explore the tourist attractions in London."

"But...we even have to share a bathroom!"

"I know, but it is only for two nights."

She had not yet told her that the bathroom was one floor down. The room costs were £35.00 per night; she had just expected a full bathroom to be included."Come, let's go and explore in the time we have before we take the train to New Castle."

Showing Sonja around London was disappointing, but ignoring it was her only option. The train trip to New Castle was better, and staying a night with Jenny was fantastic. Sonja was a lot happier. Sonja seemed to cheer up but could not pinpoint why she was so grumpy. Not like her at all.

Sonja did not like London at all. She had to admit it might have been the hotel. She took her to all the tourist places her mom visited when she and her sister were in London many years ago. Somehow, Sonja was not in a good mood.

Their return trip by ferry to Holland was also not the best. It was very windy and raining.

They took the train back from Hoek of Holland to Annemarie's place. The last few days were spent with her sister, Tom, and their three kids. Sonja cheered up, and so did she.

"I have left some clothes on your bed for you to see if there is anything you want to take home."

"Really. Oh, Sonja let's have a look."

"Mom, look!" her daughter's expression gladded her heart. How were they ever fitting all the lovely clothes in the suitcase and still not being overweight?"

"Anything you like?" her sister asked after hearing our comments from downstairs.

"Gosh, we like everything. All these outfits. Are you sure you want to give them all to us?"

"If you want them, yes otherwise they are going to a shop that will take them."

"Moppie, let's pack every heavy item into our hand luggage. It will be uncomfortable, but we might get past being overloaded."

Their suitcases were well over twenty kilos, but her sister seemed to think they would get through.

They did. What a relief. Paying for overload was not in her budget. Sonja was happy with all the new clothes she suspects were chosen for her by her sister. She was also truly very grateful for the designer outfits. Yes, she had to, despite her appearance being still vital to her. How spiritual was that?

Before driving them back to Schiphol to take their flight back to South Africa, Jan's Sister Hillygreeted them in Johannesburg. Sonja loved her, and their one-night stay before flying back to Port Elizabeth made for a nice closure to the otherwise saying-goodbye to her Dad trip.

Back Home in Walmer

Jan was at the PE airport and drove home, almost within walking distance from home. Jan seemed happy for them to return, but she sensed a change in him that she could not place.

Lately, the dreams she mostly recalled just before waking up included getting lost while travelling. She would wake up in a panic state. It was not knowing where she was. What would that mean? She kept practising getting out of her body but without much success.

The only thing she can escape to in the middle of the night is when a constant feeling of the need to get approval is somehow less, but instead, she starts to feel a kind of anger, and for what?

Sonya is Driving to Johannesburg.

"Mom, Tim phoned when you were out. He is so happy that I'm coming to stay in Johannesburg; he thinks he can stay with me in a flat while he is in the army."

"Are you sure?"

The stories she heard about army rules did not include soldiers leaving the army base to sleep elsewhere, but Tim was of a higher rank due to his college degree. Lucas would not be so lucky.

Sonja was looking forward to her assistant buying a job with Edgars. She should be proud of her, but she was sad ...Her firstborn would leave home to live in a different city far away. She was glad for Sonja because she was already twenty years old, but she would so miss her. Soon, Lucas would leave for the Army, and then she would be alone with Jan.

Lucas Goes to the Army

Seeing him all dressed in his army uniform gave her such a chilling feeling. Was it happening, sending him off to the army? They were driving him to Bloemfontein, where he would be stationed. What happened after that nobody knew?

Lucas seemed to look forward to his new life in the army, which was understandable for a nineteen-year-old, and his voluntary work at the St Johns ambulance during his high school year's school might have had some influence on the direction he would take in life.

She wondered if he would become a medic since he had volunteered at St John's ambulance.

After they dropped him off at the army base, they drove to Johannesburg to stay with Jan's sister Hilly, meet Sonja and maybe Tim somewhere, and visit Piet and Jolanda.

Leather Clothing Industry from Home

No more children living at home was difficult at first. Her clothing industry now took up the upstairs part of their home, where several seamstresses and one lady just glued scraps of leather onto a skirt panel template.

The four women sewing for the boutique orders kept her busy, but a kind of sadness took hold of her. She had to keep going, if not just for her staff to keep them employed, but she was still unsure if this was what she was meant to do from now on.

"Hendrika, quick, look out the window," Lia called from upstairs.

She was downstairs in their showroom, where she often met clients. Oh gosh, Lidia, the owner of a very upmarket boutique, had arrived. She was not in the mood to speak to her. She whispered to Lia upstairs to tell her that she was out.

"Where are you going?"

"Just tell her I'm visiting a friend."

She heard the footsteps at the front door when she got into the back garden to hide in the outside leather workroom, which she had never used anymore, now that her home industry had changed into a clothing home industry.

Why was she shaking so, knowing that dealing with Lidia took every ounce of energy from her? That woman didn't know how to accept no. She did not want only to design leather outfits for her boutique, no matter what money she offered. Her freedom to create what inspired her was more important.

Having experienced what it was like doing these fashion drawings for an advertising agency had been a good lesson. That only lasted eight months. She knew she could never work for a boss or any company. She would rather keep being a self-employed housewife.

It was nearly two o'clock, and she hoped Lidia had left.

Waking back through the garden and opening the kitchen door, she acted like she had been visiting a friend because she could never have driven off. That would have been too obvious that she wanted to escape.

Her heart sank into her shoes when she heard two female voices from the front lounge. She trembled in anger at herself for being such a coward and now had to make an excuse. She was acting as if she had just come home.

"Lidia, I didn't know we had an appointment." She acted surprised

"Your assistant said you were out, but your car was in the driveway."

"Lia, are you all finished up for the day?" ignoring Lidia's accusatory voice. Her staff only worked until 2 O'clock,

The four seamstresses came down the wooden staircase, listening to their conversation through the half-open sliding door into the hallway. She excused herself and walked out with them to their cars.

"You are not going to work for her, I hope?" Lia whispered while the others were hanging around.

"No way. See you all tomorrow. What did you tell her? Had she been waiting for me when I was away?"

"Oh, I think she knew you were avoiding her? See you tomorrow."

When she returned to the lounge, Lidia was still waiting with the pen in her hand. Gosh, now she had to be frank with her.

"Lidia, what can I do for you?"

"I want to talk some more about you designing exclusively for my boutique." taking out her cheque book.

"Oh, Lidia, you could not afford me," I told you before. I do not want to work for anybody.

"What do you mean I could not afford you? Tell me your price."

"Lidea, we will finish your order of seven leather tops and skirts next week, and we will talk again, but now I have to go back to a friend three doors down; she is ill, and I promised to come back after lunch." The lies just flooded out of her mouth.

After Lidia drove away, she only wanted to phone her estate agent friend to have coffee somewhere and get out of the house before Jan came home. Justine was out doing stocktaking somewhere, so she had better do something that would inspire her.

Exhibiting Leather Art

When everybody had gone, and she had the house to herself, her creativity with leather cut-off scraps and the leather sliding door carving project created a meditation. Her leather sliding door had two sides to it. One showed a tropical scene with flamingos, and the other was bare with dunes and a city skyline in the distance. She had entered this leather project into an exhibition to do with our environment. The sliding door would be a permanent feature downstairs from the hallway into the lounge.

Her leather wall art often expressed the philosophies she learned from being an ACT centre member. Expressing that Time was an illusion in leather was a challenge, or the different dimensions, but we are only aware of the physical reality.

Every other week, she made flower arrangements for the ACT centre and was often involved in the décor props for events. Jan would occasionally join these events, but more often, he declined.

Chapter Fourteen

South Africa is Boycotted.

Due to the apartheid law, international sanctions came into effect, and it had a significant impact on her business. Several clothing boutiques would send their orders back due to no sales. Johannesburg was bad; two clothing shops were not opening their boutiques due to the fear of looting. Here she was sitting with lots of clothes, and now that Sonja had left for Johannesburg, her outlet in the part where she ran at the local boutique was not happening anymore.

Her clothing orders came from her two agents, one for the Cape Town region and one for the Johannesburg region. They took orders from clothing and gift stores with the help of the catalogue she had made. She knew that financially, she was in trouble. The weekly salaries were vastly draining her bank account. She had to close down.

Her four seamstresses understood, knowing the showroom downstairs was entirely of returned items, including many leather jackets. They had husbands, and their income was their pocket money. But the one lady who did all the glueing of leather scraps on a skirt template was in a state; she was the only breadwinner.

Closing Down of Rapoo Art

In the last few months, when she was getting fewer orders due to the political unrest, one enterprising lady helped her out by selling her clothes and leather jackets from her gazebo at the beachfront at a low price. So that she could pay salaries, she felt terrible for one member of her staff.

She paid for a gazebo so the lady who was the only breadwinner could earn money by selling her clothing at a different beach. That lasted two months. She was no saleslady and bitterly complained.

All she could now think about to recuperate her income was to sell off her over forty leather Jackets, bags and clothes at the once-a-year Graham's Town festival months away. Art-in-the-Park was still an option, but the sales were dropping even there.

One Week at a Spa

Due to her voluntary work, she received a gift from the owner/minister of the ACT Centre,

Ten ACT members were paying for a weekly block booking at a spa in Port Alfred, two hours away from Port Elizabeth. She was the tenth person. The problem was that the dates of that week fell into the same time when Jan's parents were visiting.

"You are not going away for a week when my parents are here, no way."

"They are your parents; you can take the week off." Knowing very well, he resented having to entertain them on his own. They sat in the lounge while she was still creating jewellery from leather scraps.

"I need this break. I need to get my body in better shape. It's a gift I cannot refuse. I'm sorry for the dates that coincide with your parent's visit, but for that week, I'm not home!" her body was shaking from the energy it took to stand up for herself. Jan was furious.

Jan's Parents Visit

The week at the spa was the best experience she had for a long time. The everyday treatments, all included, were a luxury she would never be able to afford. Being in a group was a bonus, and every mealtime, which was a story, was a joyful experience. She learned a lot about herself, but the last day was somehow spoiled, knowing she needed to meet Jan's parents, who would not be happy with her for not being there. Especially his dad, who was a bully.

Losing a few kilos and feeling like a new person helped her cope with the negative vibes at home. Jan went to work again to entertain them for another week. Having no clothing business to run anymore was a blessing, but she still had a showroom where clients would visit occasionally.

She truly liked her mother-in-law, but even she was cold and distant. There was no way she could explain her interest in "New Age" topics, and she was relieved when the time came for them to leave.

Dad Passed Away

Writing in her dream journal when Jan went to work early was often the only time she could be herself. Her writing was not the best, being dyslexic, but since nobody was reading it, the memories she usually woke up with filled her with awe and writing them down created an almost new reality.

One night, she was woken up by the phone ringing in the hallway. It was around two o'clock in the early morning. She knew it was her dad.

His voice was very soft, with hardly any energy to talk, but he was saying goodbye.

"Daddy is at peace; I know, Dad. You both worry about me, but you do not. Love you lots," she whispered. Then, her mom took over.

She was crying. They were both next to each other in a hospital because mom had shingles, and her gall bladder was swelling up again due to her leukaemia, so she said.

"Daddy is gone..." she could hear the noises from the nurses that they were helping her to cope. She wondered about her sister Annemarie. Where was she?

Rejected to Sell at Art-in-the-park

For years, her sales once a month at Art-in-the-Park had been very lucrative, but ever since she started to employ people, she was not allowed to take her usual spot. Annie, the woman who had been so helpful after the fire, was the organizer.

She was told that she needed to move away from selling her leather jackets to the business section, away from the crafters.

Never mind that she had no more staff and was sewing jackets alone, Annie was adamant.

Lucas Comes Home from the Army.

For several months, she had not heard a peep from Lucas. They did not even know where he was situated in the army. He could be anywhere. After three months, she phoned the army; she needed to know where he was since a lot was still happening in Angola, although the war was over.

Not long afterwards, they got a phone call from Lucas. He told them his superior officer called him to find out why he had not written to his parents.

"I'm sorry. I needed to find out what happened to you, and I'm glad to hear from you. I do not need to know where you are, but now and then, let us know you are OK. A postcard is also OK."

"Yes, mom, sorry. I'm not allowed to tell you where I am, but I'm okay."

"Do you know when you can come home again?"

"I think soon. Many have already been discharged."

It was a few weeks later that Lucas rang the front doorbell.

"Oh, schattebol, are you home for good? How did you get home? Where did you travel from?" her joy and many questions while hugging him made him smile.

"Yes, mom. Home for good. I hitchhiked from Pretoria. "

Lucas came downstairs again back in civilian clothes. He told them horrific stories about the injuries he had to cope with. He had lost a few friends due to mines that had blown them up, killing them. His last post was in a Pretoria hospital.

"Any plans about what you want to do now? I mean, back to college or what?"

"No, moms, I will take on the job at the camping shop for now and do my bar duties in the evenings at the yacht club."

A Course in Miracles

Life took on its routine—Wednesday evening meditation at the ACT centre. Sunday, arranging flowers at the ACT centre before the service. Thursday evening, she had joined a study group on the book A Course in Miracles, held at the home of an architect in upper Walmer.

"I still have difficulty accepting that all our reality is an illusion." She shared one evening over their coffee afterwards. They had been reading each chapter of the workbook in detail.

"Sensory perception is often the most striking proof of something factual. When we perceive something, we interpret it as "objective." For real, it is seen with our naked eye!" John, the architect, replied

"Yes indeed, what is wrong with that?"

"We analyse the quality of our perceptual experiences", he replied

"Yes, we do that with our five senses of hearing, smell, seeing, tasting, and touching," Ingrid added: "I intellectually do understand that our perceptions are limited, but how do we move beyond that?"

"By accepting that our physical perception" and the "constructed perception" are of the same quality, it's just that. An illusion." John replied. She loved having conversations on this level, even if it often exceeded her understanding.

"About 10% of the time when we are awake, we are susceptible to such suppression effects, which will mislead our upcoming actions. "

This made her think of an image of an older woman, and at the same time, we can perceive the young woman. She shared her visual imagery, and they all saw it. John stood up and found the image.

"We see both", so which one is real?" John asked. Ingrid replied:

"They are optical illusions? They are images or pictures that we perceive differently than they are."

"That reminds me of Salvador Dali's paintings." she loved those evenings, even if she did not always understand the meanings in the workbook.

The Girls from New Zealand

Lucas had attracted a girlfriend at the bar where he worked as a barman. He seemed to be besotted with her and told them the horrible situation this girl Sue and her New Zealand girlfriend Karina found themselves in. They had both been travelling but would soon run out of money, so they found some cheap accommodation while finding casual jobs.

"The room they share is damp and dirty, and their landlord keeps bothering them when they have to use the shared bathroom ", Lucas shared one evening after his shift.

She was thinking of the difficult times in Australia, living at the back of a shop they managed for Jan's uncle.

"How long are they staying in South Africa?" she asked. She had met Sue, a relatively big, strongly built girl with blond, bleached hair a few years older than Lucas. She did not take to her. She found her rather brassy and forceful. And wondered if she would see Lucas in his home environment, their romantic relationship might break up

"Jan, what do you think? Shall we ask them to stay in what used to be Sonja's room? It's big enough for a short period until they get on their feet?"

It was settled. Lucas was very pleased, and Jan did not mind at all. She took to Karina. She was so different in every way. She was a short girl on the plump side, with dark wavy hair and sparkling brown eyes. One year older than Lucas. Her bubbly personality was refreshing and very different from Sue, whom Lucas loved.

Karina showed great interest in all her creative activities. She wanted to learn how to do sand art. In between her leatherwork, she still created sand-art arrangements in glass with succulents found in the fields outside PE for some gift shops and Art-in-the-Park, besides making more leather jackets for the Graham's Town festival the following year. She managed to book a double stand.

Sue and Lucas seemed close, and she tried getting to know her better, but Sue did not like her; she was Lucas' mom. There was nothing she could do about that. Sue somehow felt threatened by her. Jan was often not home. They were growing more and more apart.

Her relationship with Karina was fun. She was like a daughter, and Jan liked her as well. Together, they started to prepare stock for the big festival in Graham's Town, and Karina would help her and make some money for herself.

When Lucas and the girls were out in the evenings, she often created her timepiece jewellery from old clock pieces in the lounge. Another pastime project she had seen in a magazine while Jan was usually at work. These new projects and all her leatherwork and sand art would make for a great festival with many sales.

Mom Visiting on her Own

Her Mom had made plans to travel on her own to South Africa after a blood transfusion she had to have regularly. Being a very ill woman with an enlarged spleen and having leukaemia did not stop her. They picked her up from the airport and let her sit in a wheelchair. She was very chatty and glad to see them both.

She made herself a light grey mixed leather and suede long leather jacket as a gift. She was over the moon. She stayed in the downstairs bedroom where she and her Dad used to stay. Her Mom was missing her dad and was often very tearful, so taking her around in a wheelchair lifted her spirit.

Her mom liked helping her at the kitchen counter with a miniature leather shop display she had made over the months. It was a draw card for the Graham's Town festival next year. All her leather jackets were copies of her jacket designs made on a small scale to fit a Cindy doll.

"Gosh, you are going to so much trouble for a ten-day show?" Sue remarked. Her mom was resting outside in the shade on the reclining chair they got for her.

"I know. But it's one opportunity to sell as much as possible and attract business owners who might want a regular supply."

During her Mom's stay, she took her to the Sunday service at the ACT centre and introduced her to some very close friends, Ingrid and her husband, who were very good to her. Listening to all her stories, her mom was in her element, having such an attentive audience.

On a Tuesday evening, she joined Ingrid and her husband, along with a few other ACT centre members, at their home to study Jim Hurtak's book The Keys of Enoch. The teachings were given on seven levels, so she often found it challenging to understand fully, but she sensed the information was essential, and one day, she might grasp it all. Frequently, she regretted that she could never share anything that she learned with Jan. There was such an emptiness between them that she often wondered if he was aware of it.

Sue Leaves to go Back Home.

Sue had been helping Lucas behind the bar at the yacht club to earn her return flight to New Zealand. Karina wanted to stay. Knowing how Lucas felt about her made her sad. Somehow, she knew Sue was not his right partner, but she could do nothing about it. She wished it was Karina instead.

Karina had sewn a leather jacket for herself and was in a happy space living with them. However, she needed to keep updating her temporary residence visa by visiting her uncle, who lived in Rhodesia; she found out how to get a permanent residency with Home Affairs. She needed to employ her and prepare proof that she was the only one who could do the work she did.

It took several interviews, but they succeeded in the end.

Sue left just before the big festival event. Lucas was working for a camping and hiking shop, and she knew he was saving up to follow her in a few months. She was still hoping the distance between them would break up their relationship.

The Graham's Town Art Festival

It was primarily known as the largest festival of performing arts in South Africa. And on the African continent. Her double stand inside the most popular tent was on the festival's fringe and was full of stock: leather clothes, timepiece jewellery and sand art. Even packets of coloured sand are nicely packaged with step-by-step instructions on how to do it inside a glass.

She had spent hours drawing Karina's hand from the photos she took about each step of the way to create a sunset, a waterfall, or mountains with birds in the sky.

At Jan's work, during the evenings when nobody was in the building, and Jan had to finish paperwork or prepare for the next ship, she would photocopy her drawings and cut and paste them into a pamphlet size.

Karina loved the activities at Graham's Town. In the evenings, they would attend some shows. She had paid for the room they shared with three others in a home while the owners visited family. That was how they earned some money once a year.

Her show was a great success, and she came home with enough money to pay all her credit card debt and exchange her old Passat for a 7-year-old BMW!

Chapter Fifteen

Lucas follows Sue to New Zealand.

Six months after Sue had gone, Lucas purchased his first computer and a printer. She was impressed and often looked over his shoulder to see what it could do. To see the text appearing on a bright blue monitor screen while typing on a keyboard was amazing. It had a floppy drive where any work could be stored. In a short time, Lucas upgraded his computer, which was now called Windows 91. It now had a stiffy where more data could be stored on a stiffy disk.

Lucas was in correspondence with Sue, and he wanted to buy a ticket and ask her for financial help.

"Are you sure you want to go? You have no job to go to; what money do you think you need to get on your feet? Think about it. "

"Mom, I'm going. I have enough money for a single ticket, and Sue says I can stay with her in her family home. "

She wished she had some contact with Sue's family, but that was not happening. She remembered how her mother was to her when she told them they would again immigrate to South Africa after just being back from Australia. She said, not in so many words, but she implied that she would never make it. Her mom was angry. She needed to be supportive, no matter how she disliked the idea of him going so far away.

"OK, I will buy your computer and pay off the payments for Sonja's car now that she has left for Johannesburg. Aunty Hilly will give you cash for the car she buys for your niece. That should give you some money initially, but I know nothing about the cost of living in New Zealand."

"I will be okay, ma'ams. Do not worry. You did it, remember."

A few weeks later, with a sad heart, she waved goodbye when he drove off to Johannesburg. Jan's sister would take him to the airport. She hoped the money from the car was enough for him to find his feet.

Not knowing when she would ever see him again was difficult. It took some weeks to get over the empty feelings.

Sonja was living alone by now, and Tim would be staying with her most of the time while he was in the army.

Her training at Edgars was not what she had been hoping for. There were gruesome hours, and Tim's car that they shared between them needed constant repair. Sonja was unhappy and got herself a kitten for company in the evenings when she was alone. She felt so sad for her girly, but what could she do? Growing up was not always easy.

Creative Writing on Lucas' Computer

She had met many friends during the years when she had been giving leathercraft classes at the art college, and the one good friend she still was in contact with was Wendy. She was a secretary at PE's university. She was a great help by setting her up with a word processing program, Wordperfect 5. She used it for her work.

It took her weeks to get the hang of it and more weeks to get used to the irritating computer voice telling her she made an error. She asked Wendy if it could be turned off.

Her writing was full of spelling mistakes, not to mention her English word sentences. She learned a lot in the first few months when trying to get Liesbeth/ Tulanda's story typed the moment it came into her mind. Her character was a walk-in from a parallel universe.

Sandra's bedroom became her cutting and glueing room, now her upstairs office, while Karina moved into Lucas' bedroom.

She kept her writing private and saved it onto a stiffy drive.

The Sewing Room Became a Drawing Space.

Then, her computer needed to be upgraded to Windows 94. Her days were busy, and preparing for her learning how to draw classes that she had been planning for a while kept her busy in front of her computer. She now loved her space upstairs while Karina was doing her sand art in what used to be her outside leather work room.

When she prepared her Prickly Pear shop advertising, she first drew the artwork and used Jan's typewriter at his office at work for the text. Then, she pasted it inside her drawing and made photocopies, mostly done after hours. This time, she needed to make pamphlets for her drawing classes.

"Can I use your photocopy machine at work again?" she asked Jan during dinner. Karina was doing her bar duty at the yacht club.

"What for?"

"I want to give drawing classes upstairs; there is enough room."

She had been working on several ideas about seeing and perceiving things in reality. Being able to draw was always easy for her.

"Can you remember me drawing your profile on my Dad's ship?"

"That was a very long time ago. What does that have to do with drawing classes? I thought you were working on leather products to sell at Art-in-the-Park?"

"Oh, I still am, and Karina will sell her sand-art, but I want to use the space upstairs for giving classes. Like an 8-week course on how to draw versus how to see."

"I know you are always busy with different schemes to make money, but why not just find a 9 to 5 job?"

"I tried that, remember. " Her rapidly mounting inner rage was on the brink of being unleashed. How could Jan be so utterly insensitive?

She would also apply for the position of display illustrator artist for the museum not far away, as advertised in the papers. She was so sure about that kind of job she would love. The illustrative paintings on the walls about various historical animals from millions of years ago had always inspired her.

The disappointment at not getting the job shook her. She was so sure that was the right direction for her.

"No, I'm not interested in working for a boss. I did my best to get the museum's illustrator position, which was ideal for me" They had finished dinner.

"That is true. I still do not understand it after all the drawing and painting you did, creating a kind of portfolio." Jan was, for once, admitting her diligence to get the job.

Sonja's boyfriend, Tim, showed her his portfolio one day, inspiring her to do the same when applying for the job. She also had to include pictures of the leather carving; although she did not have many paintings and drawings, they were impressed. She had gone through three interviews. Every time, the manager asked her for more illustrations. He was trying to get her the job, and she was sure, but it was not up to him. Sadly, he called her into his office, telling her that the museum committee wanted somebody with an art degree.

She had been devastated and angry. For once, she was keen to work from nine to five on a job she felt was very suitable.

I would rather be my boss." She cleared the dinner table and did the dishes while Jan prepared his pipe.

Joris, her golden cocker spaniel, was hanging around her feet as if he knew she was going out.

"Well, I get ready. I need to prepare some pamphlets for tomorrow."

She gathered all her drawings and text printed out on the new printer. The old DOS printer was not updated enough to fit her ideas. She had already cut and pasted it into an A-5 advert-size pamphlet. She planned to market her 8-week course, including a once-a-week two-hour drawing class with a difference at the library.

Learning to Draw Through the Right Side of the Brain.

Her first students were mainly from the ACT centre. Ingrid and her husband joined her for the support and feedback she needed. Karina joined as well. She could fit in eight people at the most.

The preparations for her drawing course had been lots of work. Mostly, she prepared her drawing exercises on her new computer.

Her first class started by making every person draw their portrait by looking into the mirror. Jan had created wooden blocks with a slit where the A4 mirror tiles fitted in. She only gave them a short time to do this, and each student received a folder to store their drawing in.

The laughter that followed was funny.

"Well, if this is how I see myself, then some improvement is necessary. "Ingrid commented.

"Look at mine", Karina responded.

She walked behind them, looking at how each person had taken to this first exercise. The idea was that after she taught them how to see the positive and negative spaces around an object, it was all about interpreting the greyscale of any object in colour and many other fun-filled exercises. They didn't know they would redo their initial portrait drawing in the final class. She already knew it would be an enlightening experience when they compared their first and last self-portraits.

Her classes were starting to take off, and she added more and more fun exercises that would help get the idea across that their reality was not what it seemed. The drawing techniques were a way to open people up to themselves.

Sonja and Tim Brake, up

"Mom, our car has been stolen!" Sonja was crying on the phone. "I came late for work because of not having transport, and they just did not care; they threatened me by being laid off because of me being late. How unfair is that?"

"Oh, Moppie. And Tim, how is he getting back to the army?"

"He has not been here for a few days. He is trying to rent a car from a friend. The police say there is no hope of returning the car, but we still have to pay for it monthly!"

Knowing that Tim's parents were not financially able to help out, she wondered what she could do.

She told Jan in the evening, but he sighed, sad for Sonja and nothing else.

They had received an airmail letter from Lucas, but he had not shared all that much. Somehow, she intuitively knew he was miserable, but all she could do was pray or at least see him in her mind being happy.

Two weeks later, Sonja and Tim broke up. At first, they rented a car, but it was costly, and Sonja wanted to leave her job. Using taxis to work was not working, and she was very lonely in the evenings.

"Moppie, you learned a lot, and if that is how you feel, come home."

"Tim is distraught that I want to leave Johannesburg, but I can't stand it here anymore." The people at work are not nice, very bitchy."

"Oh, so you broke up with Tim?"

Yes, I suppose so. Tim is having fun in the army while I'm alone here."

ACT Centre Activities

She was asked to decorate the hall again for a dinner fundraising event. She had done it several times; this time, they wanted to include a children's activity about Jonas in the Whale theme. Jan would join her at those events, but he never understood how people could believe in all the nonsense they preached.

She stopped trying to change his mind. Instead, she tried to look for subjects he would not be pessimistic about. What they had in common were the children and their ups and downs.

She often joined him in the evenings, doing a lot of photocopy work for her drawing classes. Jan seemed to find it okay that she used so much paper. Sometimes, she wondered if they ever found out how much paper the copy machine went through. There were always plenty of packets in the cupboard below the copier. She always needed at least eight copies of everything in the formats she had drawn for the doodling exercises.

Remote Viewing Exercises

During her doodling meditations, she found a way to give herself answers to questions she could not ask anybody. It was an incredibly empowering experience, and she wanted to share it in ways nobody would know.

"Hi there. Are you still at your computer these days?" Jan remarked while bringing her coffee upstairs. She closed what she had been typing because when he looked over her shoulder what she had typed, he would have an unpleasant habit of reading out loud word for word what she had typed, which was often unedited.

"I'm preparing drawing and doodling exercises for the next course. It will be a more advanced course more about how we see ourselves. "

"Doodling? What has that got to do with learning how to draw?" he remarked. Joris was wagging his tail when Jan sat beside him in the dormer window seat, drinking his coffee.

She tried to explain, knowing already that he had lost interest. He got up and went downstairs to work in his garden.

The phone rang, and Jan was already in the back garden, so she had to run downstairs to answer the call. It was Cynthia, Sophie's mother-in-law, from whom she had not heard in a while. "Marga has been missing for over ten days; we are worried sick. Marga spoke to her dad on the way home from the hospital, and that is the last they heard from her, ten days ago!

"Her tearful voice was shaking from worry. Marga was Steve and Sophie's oldest daughter, who was a nurse. Her mind travels back to when they purchased their first home in Rowallen Park from them when her third child was on the way. It seemed like yesterday. Their children were growing up.

"Sophie asked me to tell you before you read it all in the newspapers because the police are now digging up their garden, suspecting foul play." Cynthia said, being very worried about her granddaughter.

"What! Why?" she replied in shock.

"They either suspect she has been kidnapped, abducted or, in the worst scenario, killed."

Gosh, She knew that Magda was her first and favourite granddaughter. How dreadful. Her body was shaking from pure shock. These things happen to other people, not to the people she knew.

She sat at her class drawing table, doodling away while holding Magda in her mind, wondering if she could see where she might be. A dreadful feeling came over her. She knew Magda had passed over, but how and why? Looking at her doodling, she saw layers of vegetation lines and a deep hole with a round ball. It told her nothing.

She could not work anymore. Instead, she had better start dinner and would tell Jan the tragic news.

Chapter Sixteen

Sonja Returns from Johannesburg

Sonja got a lift through the newspaper to drive back home to PE to bring all her stuff and the two cats she had adopted. Salvadore Dali and Picasso were their names.

Having her daughter back home was a joy, but Sonja was not happy to be back living with her parents anymore. Karine and Sonja got on very well, and soon, she fitted in, making the downstairs bedroom hers.

The relationship between her and Tim seemed to have broken up for good. She was truly sad, for she and Jan liked Tim.

Job Positions in the Paper

"Mom, will I ever find a job as a buyer? I mean shopping professionally." Sonja sighed, going over the employment section of the paper from yesterday.

"Moppie, what we can imagine, we can make real remember."

"Yea, yea, yea, look where it got me."

Looking up at a lovely daughter who looked so lost gave her a heavy heart.

She was busy finishing some timepiece jewellery for her Grahamstown Festival stall next month. Evenings were not as lonely now that Sonja was home while Jan was at work, but she knew it would not last, and she would not want that for herself or Sonja. Now and then, Karina would join her, but she often wondered if that was going to be her life from now on.

"You like what you are doing, making and selling your products?" Sonja asked, making coffee. She joined her at the dining room table, where all her clock pieces were spread out. Jan was not home, so she took the opportunity to have the space.

"The selling part is not the best, but I must make it enjoyable." Hendrica knew she loved having projects, but then she needed to expose her work to earn an income, so it was justified not to look for a 9 to 5 job.

She liked the vibe at festivals, but Art-in-the-Park was not so great anymore. Her drawing classes twice a week in the evenings were more to her liking, but what she liked the most these days was the disappearance of her character, Liesbeth, who came from a parallel universe.

"Mom, look, I never saw this yesterday morning."

"Buyer position available for the right candidate."

"Well, well, there you are. With your experience at Edgars and your college diploma, apply for it."

"I wonder where and who they are? What products are they into? I mean, it could be for hardware stuff. I mean, who would look for a buyer in PE?"

"Better find out " Joris was trying to jump onto the couch in the lounge while they were not watching him. It was getting late; Jan might be home soon, and he hated all the stuff she was busy with lying around on their dining room table.

"Mom, are you still knitting with leather?"

"Yes, I have made a few tops, but more for selling the leather yarns on a roll for people to do it themselves. Look, this is what I put together."

"Wow, that is neat. Who cut all the leather yarn? I like the packaging.

"I have people who are disabled cutting the strips from home. I deliver the scraps to them, and they cut them the way I showed them, and they get paid per kilo of cut strips. Karina and I then roll them onto a plastic stick. I found lots of those at the buyers and sellers shop."

"Joris, no."

"The same people, three of them, are also cutting the strips for the leather carpets I started. Please have a look; I started one upstairs. Karina helped me." It was already after ten in the evening. Her days were busy preparing everything for Graham's Town. She did not tell them that she knew it would be for the last time.

Joris ran in front of them up the stairs as if to say, when do I get any attention?

Job Interviews

Sonja went for a second interview for the buyer's position. The owner of a lower-income clothing store nationwide had been abroad when the advertisement was placed in the newspaper three weeks ago.

She had asked one of the women who had been working for her before if she would like to help her temporarily to finish off everything for Graham's Town. She had so much stock, leather jackets, and a beanbag from leather just for her stall. Still, together with a leather carpet display, she aimed to attract a business person with an upmarket interior business at Graham's Town. If that happened, she would hand the whole idea over to a lady who was also into leather. The agreement was that she would earn a royalty fee since she came up with the cutting and sewing idea of creating the leather carpets.

"Oh no, Salvador, don't do that. "Sonja's cat was mesmerised by the up and down needle from the sewing machine.

"Oh no! The needle broke!"

She grabbed her cat before it ran away to hide. Yes, the section of the needle was in a paw. Gently, she pulled it out, hoping the broken part would not stay behind.

"Now you know not to do that anymore." Giving Sonja's cat a big cuddle. They replaced the sewing machine needle while Salvadore ran away.

Karina went to the yacht club, and Sonja went for her third interview. They were looking for two buyers. One was for women's clothing and one for men. It was for a chain store she had never heard about. But then the one in PE was in an area where she never shopped.

She was upstairs typing away as if she were Liesbeth, living in a world like Earth, where she was known as Tulanda. She was trying to describe what she recalled from a dream. Tulanda's family home consisted of several story dwellings. The structure was made of a bamboo-type material and closed with a fabric-looking cloth. The large double-story pod homes were hanging free but attached to a mountain and joined by many hanging walkways to other homes built similarly. Tropical blue flowers were trailing between vine-like branches intertwined onto the handrails, running along many walkways connecting each cluster of dwellings.

That was it. Hendrika couldn't recall more, except that Tulanda used a tunnel-like passage to reach the top of the mountain, where she would meet a celestial being. His energy in the dream reminded her of the voice from long ago, telling her to stop smoking.

"Mom, I'm home; where are you?" Joris ran down to greet her.

"Of course, why ask upstairs? What are you busy with now?"

"Typing a dream-like scene, Never mind. And?" saving what she had typed and would go over it later.

"I got the job. Mom, I would not have believed that a clothing-buying job is available in PE. It will involve travelling to Indonesia and China!" Sonja's face beamed with joy

"Wow! I'm so glad. They were lucky to get you!" giving her a big hug.

Come, let's celebrate. I made an apple pie for your dad for after the braai he wants to have over the weekend.

Sonja's happy vibes were rubbing off on her. Her two cats greeted them downstairs while ignoring Joris, who also wanted attention.

Sonja Moves Out

Sonja started her new job the following week, and after her second-month salary payment, she was again looking in the papers, but this time for an affordable rental. Her job helped her out with transport.

She ended up renting a bachelor pad with a bathroom in Summerstrand, an upmarket suburb near the beach, not far away.

Art Festival in Graham's Town

Her BMW was packed to the brim, with just enough space for Karina in a passenger seat. A good friend would drive his Kombie with all her other products and the displays for her double stall.

They would be staying in the same house for ten nights. The evenings were a lot of fun. Three other stallholders shared dinner, chatting about the day's sales.

This time, the leather wall hangings portrayed metaphysical ideas and were more decor for her double booth. She did not mind if they did not sell.

Sonja and....to her surprise, Tim visited her stand. Sonja promised to help her out by selling some.

"Are you two back together again?" she whispered behind her counter setup."

Sonja did not reply but approached a hefty black woman looking at the many patchy big leather skirts selling for lots of money at Lidia's upmarket boutique. She still had plenty left, so she sold them off wholesale.

With utter amazement, she observed how Sonja encouraged black ladies to try the outfits. They were made for the upcoming black women's market. The outfit looked perfect when the lady came out of her temporary dressing cubicle.

Sonja added a leather waist belt and a matching handbag. And she grabbed the tall mirror they took along.

Karina was demonstrating sand art, and she sold timepiece jewellery. Her stand was always full of people, and the other stallholders were making comments about that. She was not surprised; her miniature Cindy doll boutique rested on a tall round drum, where all her stock was packed. It was a great drawcard. Many mothers asked about the price of the miniature leather jackets, but they were not available for sale. She had fun creating a miniature leather clothing shop to attract customers.

By now, several other younger black ladies were all surrounding the big mama in leather., They also wanted to try out some outfits.

"Mom, this lady is going to pay you in cash," Sonja whispered at the counter. The big woman got several rand notes out of her bra. That was the place where many women kept their money.

She paid for three entire outlets, a bag and four belts that were the last in stock!

"Wow! That was my largest sale to one person I ever made," she whispered to Sonja. "How did you know she would go for the outfits?"

"Oh, I know the type from the shop. She is a pimp, and she buys for others who pay her back from the earnings they make."

The things she learned about people during the show were fascinating.

Sonja On and Off with Tim

Sonja often came home, mostly to do her washing. Tim wanted to move in with her, but she told him she wasn't ready. Her job seemed to be what she liked. Soon, she joined the owner on his business trip to Taiwan.

Tim is job hunting and has found some work at an advertising firm, but he seems unhappy. She heard that from his parents, with whom they were still in contact. Now and then, they joined them for a braai, even when Tim and Sonja were not together anymore.

"Sonja is learning how to hassle with the Taiwanese by the sounds of it, and her boss is pleased with her," she told Tim's parents.

Karina is in touch with Sue and hears that Lucas tried to get work, but he is unsuccessful, which seems to affect his relationship with Sue. She feels his unhappiness, even when he is so far away. That must be because of the emotional cord connection they had.

Her evenings are now full of activities. Two drawing classes a week until nine in the evening and two spiritual workshops she tried to keep up with, including her Sunday morning lecture at the ACT centre. Those often lifted her spirit.

After her drawing classes, she often joined Jan in the lounge, but she would be drawn to her creative writing if he was at work. Occasionally, there was something worth watching on the TV. She loved Outer Limits, Startrek and Mr MacIver; even Jan would watch these series with her.

"How is work these days? It bothers me that you don't talk about it. " His pipe-smoking started to affect her when he had been smoking at least two pipes. It never used to, even since she stopped smoking years ago, and now that she was also getting to be of meat, her senses seemed far more enhanced. Vegetables tasted better, and being outdoors in the fresh air was far more exhilarating.

"The same as always. I'm pissed off with my colleague who always seems to be on sick leave".

"What's wrong with him?" Joris was sitting on her feet while she was doing some drawings on a small table on wheels.

"Oh, I think everything. His two boys and his wife are also often ill. They all take lots of medicines.

Chapter Seventeen

Infidelity in a Marriage

Tim's parents came around over the weekend, telling them they felt Tim would be better off working in the UK. He will never get anywhere in Port Elisabeth or South Africa.

On a Saturday in the late afternoon, Sonja came straight from work in her City Golf, which her boss bought her, but she was responsible for the monthly payments. Sonja told her that Tim was getting very needy and that she wanted to date others.

"Mom, I love Tim. It's not that, but I always need to take charge of everything."

"Charge of what? She was not aware that Sonja felt that way about him.

"In Johannesburg, I dealt with all the payments for the shopping, ... and he would ask permission to spend money on fun things, knowing there is none. "Sonja was doing the laundry, and her two kitties were hanging around her legs. She left them behind because her landlord would not allow any animals, and they were at home because they had a garden to go to.

"I see what you mean. But do you know what you want in a partner?"

"I think so. Someone who gives me space to be me, take care of important stuff, and be in control..."

"Like Daddy. He leaves you alone to be yourself and earns enough to pay for the important stuff. "

She did not know how to reply to that observation. She can't say about the loneliness in a relationship, the lack of affection, or infidelity. She knew Jan had been unfaithful. How many times and with whom, she didn't know, but there was enough evidence. It hurt a great deal the few times he admitted that he had been with others because he blamed it on her.

"I hope you find a partner that brings you true happiness. " she left it at that and went upstairs to write—allowing her character to take over...as if they were telling her about their life.

Was she withdrawing into her fantasy world? Yes, probably, but somehow, storytelling made her feel like she lived in many different realities.

Joris followed her and rested on his favourite place on the bench before the dormer window, looking out onto the street below.

"Mom, Joris' nose is all cracked." Sonja made tea for them both. Karina was colouring sand in the back garden for their next batch of sand art they would sell the following Sunday at Art-in-the-Park. During those times, she missed listening to speakers at the ACT centre.

She hoped Jan would be free on Sunday so they could drive to Schoenmakers kop, take Joris, and look for delicate crust beach shells on top of the sand-art arrangements and other bits and pieces like succulents if she was lucky.

Karina would join her if Jan were working. She asked Sonja if she wanted to come along, but Sonja had other plans.

"Have you heard anything more from Lucas?"

No, nothing. Only what Karina could pick up between the lines from a letter from Sue."

"Oh, are they corresponding?"

"Yes, and I hope she keeps it up, so at least I can learn something about what is going on. Your brother is no writer when it comes to writing to his parents. " She got bags ready for the beach trip.

"At one time, he wanted to become a fantasy writer, but it would be nice if he would more often write to us about how he is doing."

"Lucas just forgets, he is himself," Sonja replied.

Tim Leaves for the UK

A few weeks went by. They regularly held a Sunday braai with the same three couples. Tim's parents, Justine and her husband, had to escape from Rhodesia. They had not known each other there but had a lot in common. Justine's neighbours were a Dutch couple, Nelly and Jim. They emigrated to South Africa long ago, and Justine introduced them to Jan and her. They both spoke English. Jim had his own business, and Lucas worked for him occasionally.

"Tim purchased an airline ticket. He is going to join his brother in the UK."

"When is he leaving? Does Sonja know?" they were all sitting outside on the terrace where Jan built an outdoor kitchen, including a pizza oven.

"I think so. I'm sure Tim told her because he still loves Sonja." Tim's mom replied.

They had four children, and Tim was the third child. He had a younger sister. The oldest brother was an English teacher in a posh private school in the UK, and his second brother was a doctor. She knew from Tim that his parents were disappointed in him not being more academically inclined, but they supported him in becoming a graphic designer. He was very gifted but loved surfing more.

"He will miss his surfing."

"It's about time; he needs to grow up. His dad replied. "

She loved having people over but missed having nothing in common with them besides being Dutch or having children in a relationship. She always wondered what they saw in them.

Sonja Says Goodbye to Tim

Sonja came past after saying goodbye to Tim at the airport. She was tearful and confused.

"Being in a relationship with someone for well over seven years, it's normal how you feel, Moppie." She hugged her, trying to comfort her.

"I know, and I will miss him. We have been out a few times since he returned, but I did not want him to move in with me; he might have stayed if I had done that."

"I had better get back to work; I asked for an hour off to say goodbye." When she drove away in her City Golf, she felt so sad for her.

Her showroom was full of jackets and other goodies like leather jewellery bags and belts. Her friend Justine wanted to open a market shop at the Old post office and sell her collection of buttons she was a rep for and her goods. She wanted to work for herself and give up her part-time job as a haberdashery rep. Her husband was angry because he had lost his electrical repair business and was looking for other opportunities.

She had been visiting the old post office to see what Justine's little stall would look like. She wanted to support her but was worried about the security issues with her leather jackets. She had special security coat hangers that she used at the Graham's Town festival. They were very handy but not easy to take off and on.

"You have to use them; otherwise, the jackets will be stolen; believe me, I know. And what about the skirts and belts and other goods? Are you sure you can keep an eye on it all?"

"Don't worry, I will take responsibility for your stock. I know it's very valuable."

She also borrowed her carved leather old till as a showroom piece. It used to be in the prickly Pear, then at the PE Hobbies Fair a few times, and now it is in Justine's little booth.

She was still very apprehensive, mainly when Justine had employed a black saleswoman who did not seem to be all that much of a saleslady but did not want to interfere. She tried to stay positive.

The showroom looked empty now that most of the leather jackets had been sold. She wanted to keep something for the Graham's Town festival but only paid for a single stall this time. It was getting costly, and she wanted this to be for the last time.

Karina was creating a massive sand art arrangement with fantastic imagery. She got good at it. It would make her a lot of money. She was looking around for other things to do, but like her, working for a boss was not high on her agenda.

Theft at the Old Post Office

Justine was crying at her front door. Her assistant had been cornered while several guys helped themselves to the leather jackets. They forced her to hand over the coat hanger key, she claims.

"Oh no! how many?"

"I do not know. Can you come with me to have a look?"

"I will follow you." she had to tell Karina what had happened and drove off. Inwardly, she was angry at herself for allowing Justine to let her have all the stock instead of keeping it for the festival for several months.

When they arrived, her husband was there, as angry as she was, but he openly showed it. She felt sad for Justine, but why was she not at her little shop more often? So far, she had not tallied any sales in the few weeks the shop had been running.

It was a mess. Jackets were still on the floor. The salesgirl was nowhere to be seen. Her expensive coat hangers were also scattered around. Other stallholders were protecting the stall so no more goods would be stolen.

"I count seven jackets and two leather skirts, and I will not bother with the smaller items. "

"I'm removing everything. Sorry, none of my leather goods will be sold here. "

Justine was still tearful but also angry and tried to blame it on several things. She knew she also had to take responsibility for not following her instinct.

"I'm going to work out what you owe me. "

She wondered how much it would come to. Hopefully, Jan can pick up the leather goods. It was very heavy, but she did not think Justine would continue with this outlet.

"I'm not letting you get off the hook. You need to pay me back at least the cost of the labour and materials. I will let go of the loss of profit. I will let that slide."

"Thanks," Justine whispered in a tearful voice.

Her husband was even more angry when she had to pay for the losses. She would not argue with him; it was between Justine and herself.

When she had everything back into her BMW, she drove off.

Jan was also upset about the loss of money, but more to her, she allowed Justine to get all the stock for free.

"She could never have paid me!"

" You do not know that. Yes, I will pick up that heavy till. I've been carting that around to so many places; I hope this is the last time."

The rest of the week went by, and she reached a figure of R3000. It was still a great loss, but at least she would have the labour and the leather investment back at cost price.

She hoped it would not break up their friendship, but if it did, there was nothing she could do.

Magda's Body is Found

Cynthia called her one morning to inform her that they had finally found the remains of a car that had tumbled down a ravine. It was determined that the vehicle belonged to Magda, and what was left of her body was found further down. The police concluded that something made her swerve off the road, even directly after she spoke to her dad.

"Oh, how horrible. That must have been so hard for Sophie and Steve. " Yes, it was, but also somehow a relief. " Yes, she could imagine that was also true.

"Now they know that Magda must have died instantly. They can now bury her properly." Cynthia's voice was still very shaken from grief.

"They could see that her injury must have been severe. At least, that is what they were told. Their nightmare is over. "

She felt terrible for not phoning Sophie during these times. They were living in Pretoria, and they lost contact.

"Five months it took for not knowing if she was murdered, abducted or what." She thought back at the doodle drawing and looked it up. Gosh, indeed, she had been remote viewing at the time!

After her phone call, she could not do anything anymore. She called Sonja to see how she was, but she was not at work. Being so grateful for still having her around, she needed some connection with her. The phone in the hallway rang again just ten minutes later.

"Mom, may I come over? I have to tell you something, but you will not like it. "

"Oh no, what would that be? "

All she wanted to do was read a book by Annalee Skarin. No work or writing. Just read her book titled Beyond Mortal Boundaries.

Chapter Eighteen

Sonja Follows Tim to the UK

At first, she was somewhat disappointed that the book seemed very religious. It was recommended by the lecturer giving the science of mind classes.

She had read the one title: "Ye are gods" by the same author, but this book seemed full of capitalized sentences about how truth is the greatest reward in all existence. Very religious. Instead, she asked her higher self to show her what would be meaningful for her if she opened the book anywhere so she would have an answer about her own life.

"Ask, and ye shall receive. Seek, and ye shall find. Knock, and it shall be opened unto you."..... on page 316.

It reminded her about what Ingrid, her older friend from the A.C.T centre, who was very wise, had said: that a closer look at the truth behind the truth and how true the truth that we all believe in is written in William Bramley's book – Gods of Eden. They were standing at the library shelf. Next time, she had to look up that book because it was not on the bookshelf.

She knew many religious teachings were incorrect, especially the historical events full of lies, and she knew she could never explain why she felt that way. Something she had read in Rudolf Steiner's writings.

Sonja had arrived. It must be her lunchtime break. She saw her from the dormer window, and Joris was already running down the stairs.

"Hi, Mom, are you okay? You sounded so sad over the phone."

She told her all about how Magda's body had been found.

"Now, tell me what news you have. You said I would not like it." She made coffee for them both and sat down at the kitchen counter.

"Dad might be home just now. Do you want to wait?" She had a feeling that Sonja would leave. How and when, she wasn't sure.

"Mom, Tim has paid for my airline ticket so I can join him in the UK."

Wow, she had not expected that.

"What about your job? It seemed like a great job, including the travelling you get to do?"

"I know, but we have been writing to each other, and something tells me I must go. "

"So you have made up your mind. What about your flat? Can you get out of your lease?" The turmoil she felt for Sonja to leave South Africa like Lucas was almost painful.

"I found someone very happy to take over, so yes, my boss will take over my car. He is sorry to see me go but has been very understanding."

That last statement was almost a hint ...about the understanding part.

"Oh, Moppie, I'm going to miss you. When are you leaving?"

"Next week." Sonja looked at her with an expression as if to say, please approve.

"Wow, so soon. How much of your stuff are you taking with you?"

"No, I will bring it here, and hopefully, I can send it up later by ship. " Sonja was also somewhat tearful as she picked Salvador up.

"I'm going to miss you all, and my two kitties, yes and you as well, Joris?" patting the spaniel who asked for attention.

"Has Tim found work?"

"I think so, but I'm unsure if it's the job he hoped for. I will find out. I'm staying with Tim at his brother's place until we find something. "

"They both heard Jan arriving, and Sonja went up to say that she needed to return to work to finish her desk. She had been helping out with a new woman who would take her place.

"Is it okay to eat dinner with you all?" wow, that was the first time she asked that.

"Oh, Moppie, of course, and your bedroom is always here for you."

"I'm so glad you have taken it so well." Hugging her. She was unsure about that, but Sonja needed support with her decision like Lucas did at once.

When Jan came in, she said goodbye, telling him she would return for dinner.

"Well, well, what is going on? Seeing Sonja during the day, and now she is coming home to eat with us?"

"I will tell you. Are you off for the day?"

"No, a ship is coming in late tonight, so I will nap before I leave around midnight."

She told him the news about Sonja leaving for the UK. He took it well, showing no emotions whatsoever.

"Wake me up when you all have dinner. "

She had a drawing class booked for this afternoon, so she had better prepare for it upstairs. Karina and her friend went off and would not be home for dinner. Knowing it was the last time, she was glad the three would be alone. She was already missing her. What was life going to be like with just the two of them?

Forgive and Forget.

She made a lunch date with Justine now that she was free from her shop booth at the post office. Justine had paid her the amount she had told her, so they needed to go forward.

Karina and a New Zealand friend she had met recently were upstairs sewing leather scraps together to create rolls of it people could buy by the meter. She did not employ people anymore, but now and then, she would pay people part-time to help her build up stock for the last festival in Graham's Town.

"Sonja is leaving for the UK tomorrow." She met Justine at the coffee shop on Sixth Avenue.

"Oh dear, that must be hard for you. Well, I must tell you something that will cheer you up."

"Please tell me something good."

"You remember the times when we all went to bingo night, and you told everybody that you would win the R1000?

"That was years ago. Lucas was still at home."

"Well, Annie tried again to get into the University of Pretoria Onderstepoort, but she was rejected again." Her bubbly, animated friend was smiling, so more was to come.

"She was so disappointed, and then she remembered when you want something, and you see it already happening, and you feel it, and you know it...and you did win the R1000. She was going to give it a go."

"Tell me what she did?" They enjoyed their lunch, and she felt not so down anymore.

"She sat outside the office on a bench, seeing herself in a white lab coat studying animal parts and being a Vet. She put many feelings into it; what happened next was a miracle. "

"Yes, tell me more." Justine knew how to keep the momentum going.

"The office door opened, and they saw her sitting there. They were surprised but also very delighted. They had a cancellation, and the woman would phone the student who was rejected due to lack of space."

"Oh, thank you for telling me this. "Yes, that cheers me up.

Justine shared that she wanted to become an estate agent.

"How does that work? Do you have to get a diploma?"

"Yes, in time. At first, I needed to follow a licensed estate agent to learn the ropes, and I did not get paid. "

"Oh dear, what is Jerry going to think about that?" Knowing her husband was already angry about her only working part-time.

"I will never tell him. He has been in such misery ever since he lost his business. He is depressed and blames everything on me and the kids."

"He is working, not so?" they finished their lunch and walked to the parking lot.

Yes, he is, but he keeps shouting at everybody at home when he comes home from work. That is why we all avoid going home when he is there.

"Where are you kids going? Are they both still living at home?"

"Yes, they are. I do not earn enough to pay for their studies. My Dad is now living with us, which has made a difference. He has been a real support.

"Yes, he is a nice man but loves his cigarettes." Her dad was a heavy chain smoker. The whole lounge stank ever since he moved in with them.

They were parked next to each other and made plans to take the dogs to the beach early in the morning every Monday.

"Wish me luck; I'm going for an interview with a small estate agency later this afternoon."

Saying Goodbye

Going to the airport usually had good feelings attached to it, but now she dreaded it. Jan was also very quietly smoking his first pipe early in the morning.

"You are fully packed, see. I hope you have no problem with the weight of your luggage.

"Not from PE to Johannesburg, and Aunty Hilly will be waiting for me".

"Oh, she will get you through. Smart move." Being a ground stewardess for Air France at Jan Smuts Airport had its perks.

"Please let us know when you have arrived and when you are at Tim's place. Please write or call us. Unlike Lucas, who rarely lets us know how he is doing."

Sonja hugged them both with wet eyes, so she had to be strong, whispering, "We are okay, Mom."

They hung around at the airport until they saw the plane take off.

"Do you have a ship in? " she asked when they drove home. It was still early, eight-thirty.

"Yes, later. Let's first have a proper breakfast. " Sonja did not want to eat any breakfast before she left. She would have it with Jan's sister, who had taken the day off. Sonja only left Johannesburg later in the evening on a night flight.

Karina was up and about, and soon, her girlfriend arrived around nine.

"Well, now it's just the two of us." Heard anything from Lucas?"

"Only what Karina told us."

"He should have gone back to college after the army." Jan never asked her what she would do for the rest of the day. He never did. Somehow, he was not interested.

Karina went to the outside sand art room, which they now call it.

"Are you home for dinner?"

"Probably not. I let you know." He hugged her while fondling her breast. When she pushed him away, he looked angry.

"Your so-called affection never feels good. It's always sexual. Why can't you just be more compassionate? I feel just as sad and down as you must feel." She cried.

"Have more sex, and you feel better, not so emotional." with that response, he walked out of the door to his car parked in front of hers.

That was what he needed: sex, but all that was was pure lust she never felt. She knew it was lacking in her, but she had to be honest.

She has had the house to herself. Returning to her reading or writing was attractive, but she knew she better do some housekeeping instead. The breakfast dishes were still piled up, and the bedding was still in Sonja's room, so she cleaned the floors. Her depressed feeling needed some outlet, and cleaning helped.

Karina came to the back door.

"Are you okay? I waited for Jan to leave."

No, not really. I feel depressed, but I will get over it. Working helps. Jan did ask if you heard any more from Sue about Lucas?"

"Only that Lucas had casual work now and then and that she was helping her mom in her housing estate agency business. Training to become an estate agent herself."

She wondered what casual work entailed, but Karina had no idea. She had asked, but Sue had never elaborated on that.

Chapter Nineteen

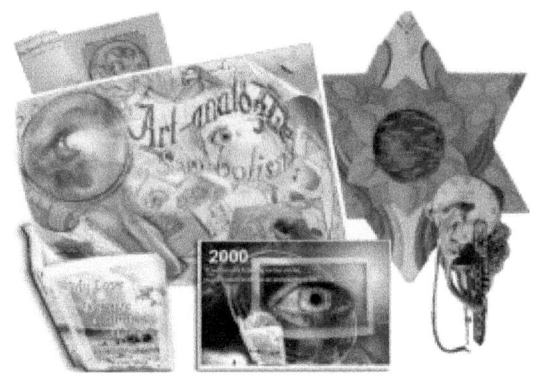

Questioning Life's Purpose.

The only friend with whom she sometimes shared her unhappiness in her marriage was Ingrid. Some friends like Justine, Piet Jolanda, some ACT friends, and even Karina might suspect that the relationship was not close, but she never discussed it. For years, she knew that something was not right. She had on numerous occasions suggested going to counselling, usually after a fight when they were alone in the house, but he only mentioned the lack of sexual intercourse.

She knew there had to be more that couples share than sex. Now that both children left home, what was left between them? She had read several books and romantic novels, knowing there had to be more between couples. She was married at nineteen but met Jan when she was seventeen. He was the only one she had an intimate relationship with, but her first experience was painful, and the six months that followed never got any better. But then she fell pregnant, much to Jan's disappointment. That had hurt her the most.

The two girls upstairs were both sewing leather patches together and chatting.

Sonja had phoned them when she arrived at where Tim was renting a room in his brother's house. The brother had a phone, but there was a restriction on it. She felt strongly that the brother was not all that happy that his younger brother got his girlfriend to stay with him as well, but that was just her reading between the lines.

"Hendrika, we are visiting some friends this afternoon, but I will be home for dinner if that is okay?" Karina asked. She was looking forward to her Wednesday afternoon, so she wished them fun with their other friends from New Zealand.

After tea with the study group every Wednesday afternoon, she stayed lingering when most had left, and Ingrid's husband left the lounge, so she had to ask her a question while helping by bringing the teacups into the kitchen.

She was still somewhat sceptical about not having to die physically, but she had to admit that the possibility was intriguing. Even not having to age was an interesting topic.

"We do have a physical human body, but we all have a Soul, and the I am is our Spirit not so? Ingrid nodded.

"How do you understand a Soul to be compared to our Spirit?" She was still somewhat confused with the two terms.

Ingrid was silent for a while and smiled.

"Well, what about if our soul, body or energy field is like a library of books, and each book represents an individual life lived."

Now that she could follow as a good example. Yes, she was thinking about all the books in the city library.

"I see, and then our spirit is the life force behind each physical manifestation" Summing up her question was a great help.

"Yes, our Soul could have a blueprint before we arrived here."

"A blueprint? You mean a script of what we want to accomplish and learn in this lifetime?"

"That's right, but sadly, the density of this world, the pain, the false beliefs, can mess up that blueprint in a pretty heavy-duty way."

Her mind drifted away to the time she had had her first encounter with a voice that she had only heard but had never seen in any way.

"I think I know now what my Soul blueprint is," she replied with an almost shaking voice."

"Then you are very fortunate, Hendrika. Follow your dreams no matter how unusual they are. You are still young enough to make the changes you might consider."

With that last statement, her husband returned to the living room, and it was time for her to leave.

On the way home, she questioned herself: Did she know her soul's purpose? Why had she said that?

Ingrid had suggested making an appointment with a psychic she knew and respected.

Visitors from Johannesburg

A few weeks ago, Jolanda and Piet asked if we were interested in a free getaway sleepover for three nights during the week in Knysna. They had been offered a four-person cottage for free in a holiday resort outside of Knysna. It was about selling timeshares, so they asked if we would join them.

"All we needed to do was listen to a sales talk, and we were free the rest of the time. "

None of us was interested in investing in timeshare, but having a nights stay over for free in Knysna was a nice break. Both their kids were living in Johannesburg nearby.

Jan had taken those days off and looked forward to the break. Spending time with them was always fun. Karina would look after the animals.

They would be here in two days, so she wanted to finish some leatherwork and prepare for a new group of drawing classes and writing.

My Creative Writing.

Stories from a Parallel Universe

Tulanda was glad to be alone with her laptop on her knees. It was almost time for a sundowner. She typed away

She had seen pictures of laptops and wanted the story to have a futuristic flavour.

Resting on her deck overlooking the vineyard in the distance gave her peace. Her mind drifted off to the events of today. She needed to type her notes on what Annelies, in reality, had experienced during their underground excursion before the physical impressions would slip away.

Her character, Annelies, was an older woman who facilitated very unusual workshops from her home to deal with our body codes of light. She had done some research on the various bodies that surround our physical form.

"Gosh, what do you think of Mom?" Hans asked out loud. He had been out jogging with the others from the group. His long, slim body was all oily from the suntan lotion he had to apply each morning. His skin was very pale, almost albino-like.

Her character Hans was Tulanda's boyfriend, and they both came from a parallel universe and had full memories of their time away from Earth.

His adoptive parents wondered why his body genetics had turned out the way they had. His unruly, almost white straw-like hair gave him an eccentric appearance, according to his adoptive mother, Annelies.

"I'm proud of her." Hans continued. " I can see her bloodline back to the Egyptian dynasty during Akhenaton. She is as pure as they come. Conceived naturally and born from her mother, just as every one of her ancestors has been. Like all the others, I do not wish to see that spoiled."

"Why would it be?"

Following her character, Hans' reminiscing was not always easy. He was inclined to jump ahead by using words that would confuse many, even herself, but somehow, the keyboard took over.

She needed to do some stage setting, so she had to build an environment around them. All she saw in her mind was a Swiss-type double-story-looking cottage near the French border. Why, she had no idea but would later edit it.

Tulanda resembled Annelies greatly, with dark, curly hair. It seemed as if the body she had grown up in was Annelies, her kidnapped child!

She started to get the actual hang of it. She was typing away. She made many mistakes, but they would have to be edited later.

"Hi there, I brought you some coffee. I've been calling you from downstairs but haven't gotten a reply."

She almost jumped back into her reality being the story writer. She saved her story and turned to Jan, who had put a mug of coffee next to her.

"Thanks, I was doing some creative writing."

"Oh, about what? Like story writing? Was that not what Lucas wanted to do? To become an author?"

"Yes, indeed, and I was very insensitive at the time by telling him first to get a diploma of sorts because writers do not make money. " she now felt she could have handled that better at the time. Lucas had even invested in books on writing short stories and dialogue, and she was now using them.

"Well, he is not a writer. We hardly get any airmail letters from him."

"Yes, and that has worried me. I strongly feel that Lucas is unhappy, but it must be me because I have the same feelings for Sonja, that she is also unhappy."

"You have a vivid imagination. Starting in a new country brings some stress, but I hope they both are young and resourceful. I'm off to the garden, and call me for a glass of wine before dinner."

She had to admit that having the freedom to do what she liked and not having to go to work was a blessing. She wished they could find something in common to talk about now that the children were out of the house.

Joris started to bark and run down the stairs; she saw Karina who had borrowed her car.

Friends from Johannesburg

On Saturday evening, at dinner time, Jolanda and Piet arrived. She had prepared the back bedroom for them. They talked about the kids. Their baby girl was pregnant!

"Wow! You will soon be grandparents. "

So much has happened since they met on the passenger liner sailing into Rotterdam, where they have spent most of their time together. Over several years, they had spent some camping trips together with the children. Spending three nights in a bungalow in a holiday resort just outside of Knysna was the first trip just with the four of them without children. Piet wanted to take his car because he planned to look around in that area for land to build on.

It reminded her of when Jan wanted to buy a nursery in Plettenberg Bay, near Knysna, but by then, she already knew that she did not want to start a business with him, knowing it wouldn't work. The children were both in high school and didn't want to move. Ten years earlier, she would have been keen.

Jan was interested in Piet's plan, but Jolanda was not. She did not want to leave Johannesburg and be away from the kids

She listened to them with divided attention. If they only knew where her mind was, what she was interested in. More and more, she was feeling separated from them.

Piet wanted to know what she had been doing now that she had the house to herself.

"Tomorrow, being Sunday, I have my last Art-in-the-Park event. I hope to sell at least one jacket, but times are not what they used to be."

"Oh goodie, I would love to see what is all for sale. I love craft markets. " For her to set up her gazebo so her jackets could hang on the frames had become a chore. For the last few times, the fun had gone out of it. She had outgrown craft markets.

"Have you heard anything more from Lucas?" Jolanda asked.

"Yes, last week we got a letter with photos. I was shocked at how thin he looked. He has broken up with Sue and hired a room from a single mom with one child. He met her at a party. Sue and Karina know her."

She knew that Lucas had gone through a difficult time emotionally.

"And Sonja?" Piet asked. They were having a late-night drink after coffee in the lounge.

Jan never volunteered an answer, so she told them that Sonja and Tim moved out of his brother's house and rented a room in someone's home in London. The time they had spent with Tim's brother while trying to earn some money doing all kinds of part-time selling jobs had been hard on both of them

The following day, the four helped her set up her Gazebo. Karina had a shift at the yacht club, so she could not join her.

She still had many leather jackets to sell, and the money would be handy. Justine would also be there with her buttons; she tried to sell on others' behalf. She far more enjoyed being an estate agent.

She watched out for customers while the three of them walked around the park. She sold two handbags and a belt. That was it. She would keep all her stock for the last Graham's Town festival after Easter to clear out.

Knysna

Their outing was an experience. After moving into the bungalow, which was very lovely, the two bedrooms were on both sides of the lounge with an open fireplace. They had brought drinks and snacks for the evenings. During the day, they would eat out.

Jan insisted on having sex, no foreplay whatsoever, and so she just let it happen. Not want to spoil their short get-together with friends.

He usually fell asleep afterwards so she could read the one book she had brought along. Life on the Cutting Edge by Sal Rachele

Joining a Port Elizabeth writing club

Weeks passed, and she gave more and more time to creative writing on Lucas' computer. It was going very slowly. Every sentence was complete of mistakes. She could not decide about her character's name, Liesbeth or Tulanda.

The vivid dream she wrote in her dream diary was now becoming part of her character Tulanda's story. The setting she placed where her mother came from.

Leersum – Utrecht – Holland

The dream she woke up with this morning lingered on. Liesbeth was sure that was because of the exciting emotions of happiness. It was as if today was her birthday, and someone had organized a party for her. Slowly, the memories were slipping away, and instead, the traffic noises outside the bedroom made her look at the clock. Gosh, she had to hurry. It would be a sunny day; glancing at the sky through her bedroom window. There was a mountain in her dream, and she was climbing to the top. There were no mountains in Holland, and what she remembered of the scenery in her dream looked like nothing she'd ever seen.

For now, she has kept short pieces of writing together. She still had no idea where her writing was going. She learned a great deal from Lucas' book on how to write a novel. If only he would still pursue this as a hobby.

Joris joined her next to her computer on the dormer windows bench seat. Nobody else would now sit there; it was full of his hair. Writing seemed to take a lot of mental energy, so she better give it a break.

Once a month, she joined a writing group, hoping to learn from other writers, but she was still far too intimidated to enter any of her writings. Even when they gave consignments, she rarely handed hers in. It was always the same people who did, so they did not miss hers.

Star of David Wall hanging.

On days when nobody else, like Karina and her friend Lisel, was sewing upstairs, she started creating wall hangings with many leather scraps to express metaphysical ideas. One wall hanging had an Egyptian flavour. At the same time, it was a lamp. She would enter this in a local art exhibition where everybody can enter works in all media.

The minister at the ACT centre had also given her an assignment—a leather art wall hanging big enough to be against the back wall behind the Sunday speakers. At first, she had drawn an idea for the artwork in leather before she started. They liked the idea of the twelve petals of the heart chakra with the planet Earth inside.

Jan helped her by making a wooden Star of David frame where she would mould seven colours in leather portraying the colours of the rainbow it was a considerable project. It was well over two meters across.

The weekends were mostly spent outdoors entertaining friends. They had an ideal entertainment patio with a built-in braai, a pizza oven next to the swimming pool, and Jan's big birdcage with ringneck parrots further down. Tim's parents, Justine and her husband and their Dutch neighbours were regulars.

Salvador is Run Over.

She was in the kitchen preparing salads when the front doorbell rang. A stranger greeted her, asking if she owned a tabby cat. Salvador was a tabby cat, so she followed him on the road. He was very sorry not to stop in time to avoid the cat. She hoped it was not Salvador; she was very attached to him, but it was. He always had a kink at the end of his tail from when he was a kitten when a door slammed and broke it.

She picked him up and brought him home, waking with him in the back where everybody had a good time around the fire.

By this time, she was crying, and both Justine and Nellie comforted her, but her husband Jim remarked, oh well, it's just a cat! From that moment, she could not stand him.

Jan told her to put him in the back garden. He would bury it later, asking for the salad in one breath.

She ignored them all and went to the back garden. She found an empty box and a spade and dug a deep hole in the corner right at the back behind the vegetable patch where Snoopy was buried. Justine joined her. Nellie had made an angry remark to her husband. So that was the end of their weekend braai party.

Lucas Might be Coming Home.

Lucas has been living with Sue's friend for a few months now. He had written several times about his on and off jobs, one of which was with a building firm. The woman he was staying with had a seven-year-old girl, and he had saved up for a return ticket to London. He would remain with Sonja in the UK and hope to earn a plane ticket back to South Africa.

She and Jan were delighted to read that news, and so was Sonja, who already had jobs lined up for him.

Then, shortly after the first letter, another airmail letter arrived.

She thought he had a landlady, but she didn't know that he had become involved with her and that she was pregnant with his baby.

Four months into the pregnancy, she discovered Lucas had plans to come home. Then she told him.

Lucas, being who he is, decided to change his plans. After some thought, he felt he had to bring up his child, so he cancelled his airline ticket.

In a lengthy letter, she responded to him, expressing her understanding of his situation and acknowledging his need to take on certain responsibilities, which she believed to be valid. At the same time, she pointed out that he could also fulfil those responsibilities financially. The letter also conveyed their deep sadness at the prospect of not seeing him return to London and then to his home.

Sonja was very upset and called her. By now, she was no longer living with Tim. They had broken up, and Tim had gone to the USA to sail on wealthy people's yachts as a crew member. He wanted Sonja to join him and see the world before settling down. Sonja was not interested. She had just landed a buyer's job at a large department store in London, so she moved into a room and shared a bathroom and kitchen at a friend's place who had inherited a house.

Days and Evenings Filled with Activities

Her days were full of leatherwork, home art classes, and creative writing. In between, she still went to the ACT centre on a Sunday morning. A lady from the USA had been lecturing on the Enneagram personality type topics for the last three afternoons, and she attended all of them and purchased several books on the subject. She was very attracted to her way of explaining it.

One evening during the week, she went to a meditation group at the ACT centre for one hour after dinner and on Thursdays for two hours to her A Course in Miracles study group in Walmer. One afternoon, Hendrika joined another study group on The Keys of Enoch with Ingrid at her home. She had also enrolled in an astrology course one morning a week with a well-known astrologer. She went to a Pilates exercise class early in the morning because of a lower back problem.

Jan often complained about never being home, but she always was just after nine. He was usually not home due to his work. Her activities and interests kept causing friction between them, and she knew he was not happy either, but she needed to keep busy to keep her sanity.

Gradually, an ascension plot was formulating in her mind. More and more, she realised that somehow this was why she had come into this incarnation, but why she had to do that through writing was still intimidating.

More and more dream visions from years ago made much more sense. She had written down some, and rereading them made her remember the visions as if they were her latest dreams.

The Terra Papers.

Margriet was a fantastic ACT centre speaker. She would be giving a weekend workshop that she was keen to attend. Jan had a ship in, so she felt relieved. It has proven to be a very controversial topic. It's all about aliens.

Robert Morningsky, the author of the Terra Papers, claimed to have connections between alien beings, Native American lore, and every single mythological and religious tradition on Earth. Margriet used a drop sheet she had prepared about the Orion wars millions of years ago to do with the History of the Human Holocaust and that Humanity originally came from the constellation of Lyra.

The drawings Margriet had copied from the manuscript were helpful, but at the same time, there was so much she covered that remembering it all was impossible.

The Terra Papers were unprofessionally printed by an old-fashioned DOS printer and ring bound, but she purchased them anyway.

Ingrid remarked on the works by Zecharia Sitchin. Margriet seemed to know his work, and together with Ingrid, they were comparing the writings inside his book The 12th Planet, which was on the ACT bookshelves for sale.

After the lecture, she looked up the content of this book, read on the back cover about the Sumerian civilization, and presented millennia-old evidence of the existence of Nibiru, the home planet of the Anunnaki.

It was all new to her. She had never heard about Nibiru, but all the latest information had stimulated her inquiring mind, so she now had to let it all sink in. Now that she believed it all, it needed more profound intuitive research.

Start Writing the First Chapter of a Novel

Her last meeting at the writing club was enough for her not to share her topic. She had shared some short stories, but the response was not all that positive. They kept suggesting that she needed an editor.

The first chapter of her novel would be a considerable challenge, but she wanted to enter the South African yearly competition, so she aimed to go at it.

She had already created a character script and what each person looked like in every way and personality-wise according to the nine types on the Enneagram.

She had learned a lot from reading Lucas's books about the stage setting. Her novel had to be in Holland. She knew that would be the best.

Her main character was Ingrid. The intent behind her novel was all about the five stages of awakening, but it also had to be a romantic novel. She knew that genuine close relationships exist and wanted to explore this kind of union between two people in great detail through storytelling. The word count for the first chapter had to be at least 1500 words, but hers kept getting longer and longer, so she learned how to shorten it every time she read over it.

A Surprise Visit

The preparations for the last Graham's Town exhibition would have to be a success. Hopefully, she would earn enough money to travel to the USA with the ACT centre members.

Her mixture of products ranged from a beanbag in leather to her Cindy dolls leather jacket shop display, this time with tiny jackets for sale! Karina would not do the sand art again. She made some leather products independently and would help her in the stall. Her friend would soon be leaving to go back home to New Zealand.

The phone rang, and Joris was racing down the stairs. A man's voice asked who she was and told her he was Sonja's friend from the UK. He had promised to pick up her cane coffee table to fit it into his container! She was so flabbergasted at his story she did not know how to reply.

Not ten minutes later, the front doorbell rang, and when she opened it, she saw a short bald man in a tracksuit with one arm tucked into a pocket, as if he only had one arm.

"You phoned just now? "

"Yes, I would like to take the measurements of the coffee table. Do you mind?" With that comment, he stepped inside and looked into the lounge where Sonja's cane table was.

"I have no idea how to measure it, but Sonja never told me someone was coming for it?"

He did not reply but asked her to hold the measuring tape because he only had one arm. Following this strange man 's instructions, she felt silly and saw Karina and her friend looking down over the top railing. That was a warning that something was wrong, but the front doorbell rang again. She opened it up and looked into a movie camera.

"Moppie!" She shouted in absolute surprise.The laughter that followed brought Jan into the house when he heard all the commotion.

For a moment, she looked at where that strange man had gone. He had disappeared!

After many hugs and kisses, he suddenly appeared in different clothes but with both arms, smiling while encircling Sonja, clearly showing they were a couple.

Getting used to the Older Boyfriend idea

They were a couple, but she could not grasp why Sonja would fall for such an older adult as a partner.

"Mom, we did not know how to introduce Frank. I know you both would not accept him as my boyfriend easily, but he makes me happy." Sonja was trying to explain that she was serious about this guy when they were alone.

"How old is he? What is his background? He is used to getting his way, which shows in his mannerisms. Yes, he seems very charming, but...Moppie, why?"

She could still not get over it and how Jan would react.

"Where, what bedroom ... she whispered when Frank carried their luggage in from the hired car."

What used to be the showroom had now turned back into a bedroom again. Jan had done the carpentry work. It had two single beds in it. It had two single beds in the room, and most of her leatherwork was stored upstairs in what used to be Lucas's bedroom.

"This room is fine, Mom." She told Frank to put their suitcases there. Sonja told them they met four months ago on London's underground when she was going to work. At first, she was not interested, but he kept pursuing her using flowers and chocolates each day delivered to her work.

All she could think about was that Sonja was arm candy. He was very wealthy—the sadness at facing them as a couple was hard.

When they were on their own in their bedroom, Jan showed his disgust by saying, "I did not bring her up to become a prostitute!"

"Shhh... I do not want Sonja to hear you say that." Let's give him time to show us how they are together. I know that it must be his money that persuaded him to get Sonja, and by what I heard, it took him weeks of pursuing her before she agreed to have dinner with him."

"So, he used his money to buy her, and she fell for it! I'm disappointed."

"Well, being pursued by a man who owns a helicopter while Sonja was lonely and struggling to make ends meet was unfortunate. She was very vulnerable, and he knew it. "

Frank took them out that same evening and the two following dinner times. During the day, Sonja showed him around in their hired car. He was charming and hilarious, making Jan even laugh. She had little time to talk privately and felt that Frank ensured that.

They had been in South Africa for a week before arriving in PE. They drove through the garden route from Cape Town and stopped at every major holiday resort. She had to admit that Sonja seemed to be impressed by his ways.

When they said goodbye, she felt somewhat hollow and sad.

Chapter Twenty

Their First Grandson

Lucas sent photos of him holding up his baby boy. He looked happy and proud. They had to admit that staying to be a father was a good choice for him. He had a permanent job at an engineering firm, but as what they had no idea. Lucas never elaborated much in his letters.

Sonja phoned regularly, and Frank bought a flat in London for them both with a view over the River Thames. Frank also talked her into quitting her job, travelling between his other estates, and helping him with his business. They seem to live a lifestyle Sonja had craved until the day she phoned.

"Mom, I want to return to work, earn money, and know what I want to do."

Sonja had seen an advert in the paper from United Airlines looking for candidates to be trained to become an air hostess. She had applied with 3000 other girls.

"You know what to do. See yourself wearing their uniform from now on wherever you go. Feel the emotions when people look at you wearing it. Imagine walking in the aisles of a plane. Keep that intent, and you will get in.

Sonja stayed in London in their flat, and Frank encouraged her to apply for it. She was happy that he had done that, but then he had four grown-up children from his first wife, so he must have understood Sonja's need to be independent.

She was accepted and flew to Chicago for her 8-week training while Frank paid her money to live on. They both knew that they could never support her financially that way, so they were grateful to Frank.

A few months previously, she had entered the first chapter of her novel into the countrywide competition but had never told anyone at the writers club.

After much editing with lots of help and suggestions, she learned a lot, and now her novel was almost finished. She never thought about it anymore and continued with her first novel, chapter-for-chapter editing and editing.

At one time, she had asked Jan for help reading her writings aloud to hear how it all sounded, but he was so demeaning and embarrassing by reading her work that she never asked again.

Instead, she asked one retired ACT centre member, Ria, who was also one of the speakers and an English school teacher in her days, if she could go over her writing to guide her.

Ria asked her to print out what she had written so far, and she said she would return it to her.

The Internet Arrived in Port Elizabeth.

What a change that made in her life. She had to set up a connection and learned to connect via dial-up. It was costly, so she restricted herself to thirty minutes a day. This new learning curve took most of her time at the computer while her leatherwork lagged.

The following Sunday, she was looking forward to meeting Ria again, wondering and somewhat apprehensive at the same time.

Ria saw her arriving at the ACT centre and walked toward her, smiling.

"Hendrika, I'm very impressed by your content, but it needs a lot of editing, and I will do it with pleasure. I see that as one of my soul gifts for free!"

She was so happy to hear that response, and they arranged for her to come over once a week for an hour, which they would spend together editing every chapter.

Winning an Award

One morning, when Jan was going to work, and Karina was writing letters home, she received a phone call from Johannesburg asking if she was the writer of the novel's first chapter titled MENTAL TELEPATHY.

She was silent for a moment, wondering why she was asked. She replied, "Yes," in a timid voice. She was almost too scared to be told something she would not like.

"Congratulations, you came first in all the entries in our country."

That was so unexpected that she had to sit down.

"Are you still there?"

"Yes, Yes, I'm sorry, I'm so overwhelmed. Thank you so much for this news.'

They told her when and where she would receive the trophy, and she would keep it for a year. All she wanted to do was tell everybody her good news, especially Jan!

She first called Ria, who was delighted for her.

Surfing the Internet

Weeks after she received her trophy, she was planning another far more daring scheme. She wanted to travel to attend workshops by professionals.

She looked up several authors Like Diana Cota-Robles because she loved her books. She read that the next conclave would be held in Colorado Springs in the USA. Somehow, she knew in her heart that she wanted to attend it, especially knowing that several members of the ACT centre were planning a trip to the USA to participate in the Science of Mind Congress in Portland.

Living our Purpose.

She was becoming increasingly like a globe trotter but through the internet. Winning her literary prize had given her the confidence she needed.

Having an email address was also helpful. Every morning she would check her inbox. Last week, she found an interesting website titled The Spiritual School of Ascension. SSOA. By Karen Danrich (Mila) It was all about channelled material, and they held conclaves.

Reading about the possibility of ascending our physical body into a light body that ageing is a disease and that genetic scientists from other worlds have manipulated our DNA was like an addictive tonic. Hendrika knew she needed to become a member. Knowing that this was her soul's purpose, to write about the last years during the end times that are coming for humanity to wake up to the truth, was still daunting, but she had faith in the support that would come when needed.

She knew it would be a lonely road for her, and she had lingering doubts that she could do it, but she needed to focus on her intent.

Found a Literary Agent for her First Novel.

Ria had been fantastic, making her rewrite most of her chapters, but some parts felt wrong. Her characters had lost their soul. That is what it felt like, but she did not have the heart to tell her, so she was looking online for a literary agent, having learned that most publishers at that time only worked through an agent before taking on a manuscript.

She found one online. She lived in Durban. It would cost her. page for page, but somehow, she needed more understanding about writing fiction.

Joining the ACT Centre in the USA

Her bank account was growing due to the sales on the beachfront with the woman who had sold products for her before and the money from her drawing classes so she could finance the travel itinerary she had all planned.

For weeks before, she had prepared Jan that she had saved money to join the group in Portland to attend a Science of Mind Congress. Hotels and everything else was included in the booking. She told the travel bureau that she would not return on the same date because of the Congress in Colorado Springs but that travelling to the USA in a group had saved her a lot of money. She showed the bookings she had already done ahead of time.

She was going to tell Jan the rest of her itinerary, but he was already angry with her. Not that it was costing him a cent.

"Why must you add other activities to the already busy schedule?"

"I would normally not attend the Portland Congress, but it's not what interests me. The return ticket from New York to Johannesburg and Port Elizabeth is much cheaper."

"So, what are you doing in the meantime?"Jan was angry, and he got up from the dinner table. She had cooked his favourite special meal, but that made no difference.

"Tell you what. I do not care. "

"I'm leaving in a week; why can't you for once support me in what interests me? I always support you in your garden activities?"Jan never replied.

Jan Drives Her to the Airport.

They were all there. June, the minister had grouped them in pairs. They would share the hotel and dinner costs and any other included activities. She didn't know that and was somewhat disappointed with who she had to share the trip with. She looked forward to the whole adventure and would make the best of it, knowing her real trip was starting after they returned. Not many knew that.

They first landed in New York after a 17-hour flight. The one night in a hotel was a short affair because they had to change within the hour to attend the musical Cats, and then the following day, they flew to Portland.

The musical was impressive, but she was so cold, the theatre was freezing, and she had difficulty staying awake. She hardly saw anything. The following day, they were taken to New York airport by taxi to fly to Portland via Dallas, where they would change planes.

The food on the domestic flights was very artificial. It was handed to them at boarding in a brown packet.

Margriet was a speaker at the Congress, so that was an honour for the SA group. They all held her in high regard.

The week in Portland was an exciting experience. She met several speakers they all knew from the books they carried at the ACT centre.

She met a Dutch lady during a break in between speakers who lived in Portland and who invited her to her home. She asked the others if they would take care of the partner she was hooked up with, but the woman was not pleased. She was very clingy and insecure.

She went anyway. Her agenda was so different; she needed to learn so much on this trip, and having a person to babysit was not an option.

She visited the largest bookshop in the USA (so she was told) independently. Her partner was still sulking, so she left her in their hotel room.

She bought several books; some were second-hand but in excellent condition. Paying for them, including the packing and shipping back home, was a tidy sum, but she could not carry that on her extended trip

The flight to Miami was ok. She was sitting on her own. The woman with whom she had been partnered sat with someone else, who was not all that pleased. Only one ACT member knew about her itinerary, and she winked at her to ignore them. She was the daughter-in-law of the minister. She was very outspoken and direct, which she admired. She was from Australia, and they got along very well.

"I'm jealous of you, having the guts to go on your own after this stuffy group," she whispered when they arrived in Miami.

"Yes, I can see that you would love to do what I'm going to attend. I will tell you all about it when I'm back home."

"You had better do that. Have fun at the same time."

If only she had been partnered up with her, that would have been so different.

Disney World was impressive but boring at the same time. She was used to the Efteling in Holland. There was no comparison. Everything was so artificial and clinical, unlike the creations of Anton Pieck, her favourite Dutch artist.

While walking back to their hotel, a few raindrops seemed to scatter people. Suddenly, people were wearing plastic raincoats and running to get inside. She had never experienced a monsoon type of cloudburst. It was as if someone opened the tap in the sky. They were all drenched.

The following morning, she told her hotel companion she would not fly home with them. She had been painful, remarking whether she had left clothes on her bed or her suitcase was not in the corner like hers.

"Where are you going?"

"My bus takes me to Virginia, where I plan to visit the Edgar Cayce Foundation. I will be staying at a backpacker's accommodation."

"All on your own?"

"Yes, I have other interests, and I am doing more research on my novels". Hendrika had silenced her with her comment, and that was okay. She was used to not having any support or encouragement, and her years of experiencing a lonely and empty marriage had made her more independent. She had learned that she did not need approval from others.

Saying goodbye was almost laughable. Most had no idea why she was not travelling back with them, and Hendrika could imagine the following talks about her further travel plans.

Her emotional feelings and deeper anxiety were heightened during her long bus ride, but it gave her time to sleep.

Her main event was to join the workshop of Diana-Cota Robles in Colorado Springs, but the times were out. She needed to spend five weeks somewhere before her main event would start. Her first week was taken up exploring the Edgar Cayce Foundation.

Virginia Beach

When she arrived at the backpackers and saw where she had to sleep, she realized that due to her heavy period, privacy was more important. Therefore, she asked if a room was available.

"Only our most expensive room."

She paled at the cost for a week, wondering if she would run out of money on her credit card when she arrived in Colorado Springs.

"I will take it for five nights."

The room was lovely, and it had a fridge. That was a bonus in the tropical heat.

"Hi, I've not seen you around. Just arrived?" a woman asked her at breakfast, which consisted of a white bun with a slice of processed cheese. She had a pleasant face younger than her,

"Yes, last night from Miami, and you?"

"I'm from New York. I have taken a week off from my studies. What is that accent from? Are you German?"

She explained where she was from and being Dutch. Marion wanted to share her company, which was fine, but she explained why she had come to Virginia. They spent the rest of the week together. Marion was studying to become an environmental lawyer and earned money as a dog walker. She had booked the smallest room she had ever seen, and together with one other woman from Ireland, who only worked for eight months of the year in a factory to be able to travel around the world staying in backpackers.

She took them both along to the Edgar Cayce Foundation, walking through a forest with the help of a map. She loved their company and learned a lot about what it was like to be free to do what you wanted.

Marion purchased lots of books at the foundations. They all joined some short film lectures about the life of Edgar Cayce.

When her time was up, and a taxi took her to the airport for her flight to Boston, they became real friends and shared contact information.

Boston

In Boston, she stayed in a women's hostel, which was very cheap. She had a tiny room by herself, but it had a horrible smell left behind by a heavy smoker. She walked around, having to save money as much as she could and lived on small takeaways spread over lunch and dinner. It was a beautiful city.

Seven days later, she took the Greyhound bus to visit her sister-in-law in Montreal for two weeks. From there, she would fly to Colorado Springs to join Diana-Cota Robles's ten-day workshop held in a 5-star Hotel.

Montreal

She had not been aware that they mostly spoke French at Jan's sister's home and with the friends who came over, so she spent much time reading alone.

Colorado Springs

Her arrival at the luxurious hotel in Colorado Springs was a huge change compared to where she had stayed. Thank goodness everything had already been paid for online, so she had to be mindful of the expenses for dinners that were not covered. Her hotel room was huge, with two double beds. Was she going to share the room?

Sure enough, it was not long before a knock on the door announced another jolly, friendly woman from Australia; she took the other double bed. Another knock and a third woman joined them. They discovered that they also shared a double bed with a stranger! Her bed partner came from Texas. The other came from Ireland.

The first night before the congress started was awkward. She held onto her side of the bed so she would not touch her bed partner.

The first day of the Congress was an experience. Diana used the sharing of rooms or, in some cases, a bed as a workshop. There was lots of laughter, and over a hundred people from all over the world attended. The lecture room was incredible, and Diana's amazing voice stirred many hidden traumas within them all. A lot of inner learning about themselves was profound.

The following days were all amazing; they went river rafting to challenge their fears, visited a large rock and boulder park to learn about true silence, and went up by train to the top of a mountain to face heights; it was altogether unforgettable. The best investment she had ever made and their fun with the four of them in one room was a cherry on top.

She had lost at least five kilos because of the time spent living on little food. Whenever she needed to draw $100, she was relieved it was still coming from the ATM.

They shared addresses, hugging each other. And they all went on their way home.

She had booked her return flight to New York to return to South Africa with a connection to Port Elizabeth.

Return Home and Separate from Jan

On the plane home, she knew she needed to decide to separate from Jan. How she would do it was still unclear, but just carrying on with her routine was impossible for her anymore. Her spiritual journey had to become her first propriety. She was still on cloud nine, arriving in PE, so she had to keep her spirits up while facing Jan's angry comments.

Jan was at the PE airport, and the first thing he said was

"You look dreadfully skinny. What happened?"

She was surprised because being on a high from all the spiritual upliftments should have been seen as a positive reflection.

Jan was not interested in hearing about her trip; he told her that being away for six weeks was a pleasant experience.

The negative onslaught from him after her joyful trip was a punishment for her selfishness, and Jan's draining energy became apparent. Yes, she had followed her intuition, knowing it annoyed Jan. Was that selfish?

She took her car to visit Ingrid; she could not stay home, and somehow, she needed to break away from Jan to sort out what to do.

"You mean separating from Jan," Ingrid responded. She already knew she had to leave him, living in the same house but in different bedrooms for a start, which might not be enough.

"If that is in your heart, go for it. If I were your age, I would have, but I'm too old and know my time is not over." Ingrid replied, knowing her husband was pottering in the garage.

They hugged each other, and enough was said. This woman was her spiritual mother and the only person she would miss if she left Port Elizabeth.

Ingrid and her husband had run a hotel at the Hogsback for years, and she knew of a friend looking for someone to take over the rent of her cottage while she was visiting family.

It was arranged that she would arrive the following day and stay at the Hogsback for eight weeks.

Driving home, she had not yet unpacked her suitcase, so she just put it in the boot with her computer, books, more clothes, and a few leather goods and wall hangings she might sell at the local market.

When Jan came home in the evening, she cooked a meal but was not hungry.

I'm leaving tomorrow morning for the Hogsback. I'm staying there for eight weeks to sort out my life. Our marriage is over, and we need to make some decisions.

Jan never said much, and Karina was out most of the evenings, so they ate their meal silently.

Moving to the Hogsback for Eight Weeks

Driving up to the Hogsback, a magical world of mountains and forests high up on the Amathole mountains, took her into a shifting mood. She was not the same person she used to be. The things she once put up with are now becoming unbearable. Before she remained quiet, she was now ready to speak her truth.

She listened to the music she had purchased at Diana's congress, lifting her spirit. The last time she visited the Hogsback was with Jan and Roy Littlesun, a speaker from the ACT centre. Jan tolerated him during his stay in PE at their home because he spoke Dutch and was willing to share a steak on the braai. Although Roy was an Indonesian and lived in Amsterdam, he was sixteen and brought up with the Hopi Indian tribe in the USA. Roy had been invited to a medicine ceremony, and she offered to take him there. Jan volunteered to drive the car.

The hairpin bends up and up, leaving the lower valley with orange farms behind. Now, it feels like she is moving into a new reality.

She was looking forward to carrying on editing her novel, studying her astrology file, and just being in a meditative mode in the forest on her own. There was a landline but no internet, so she needed to find out if she could live independently.

Her cottage key was at the Hotel, and at the same time, she asked the manager if some of her wall hangings could be on display.

She knew of one mutual friend, Anna Holmes, so at least she could visit her if being alone was getting to her.

Weeks passed, and then she got a call from Justine saying that Jan, Karina, and herself were planning to visit over the weekend. Hoping she has space for them.

Anna helped with two single matrasses, and there was a couch.

Her quiet life suddenly changed into jolly, happy activities, and in the evenings, they played games, which Justine had taken along.

Jan tried to get her to share her bed, but she was uninterested. Then he had handed her a letter she would read after they left just after lunch.

The visit had exhausted her so much that she wanted to sleep.

She dreamed that someone was giving a lecture. "It's essential to end a relationship with grace and kindness for starting a new future."

She heard herself asking when one knows when to break away for good with a partner.

"If you want to end a relationship with as much dignity, humanity and kindness as possible, then that is what you must do."

She was with a group of people listening to a lecture about marriage and divorce.

"You mean making up and then being honest, kind and considerate but still wanting to separate. "The idea to start all over again in every sense of the way was an unbelievable task.

"It will free you by acting in good conscience, even if you are the only one behaving well." With those words, she woke up.

Jan's letter was still unopened on the coffee table. He proposed to pay her a sum of money each month to live on. While they each went on their way, she would have no claim on the property. Thinking that the house in both names would now be his alone was unbelievable.

Her hurt went deep, and she then went into meditation to ask for guidance. While dozing, she asked to feel having an in-love feeling as proof of what she needed to do. She had to return and make up with Jan before she would be free.

When she woke up again, she felt like she was different. Her emotions were in turmoil. All she wanted to do was go home. She packed her car with all her stuff, cleaned the cottage, wrote a letter to Anna and the cottage owner, and left the keys at the Hotel. All in one hour. It was well past seven in the evening.

Returning Home to make up with Jan

Driving in the dark was never fun, but she hoped she was not too late. Her intuition told her that Jan would bring another woman into the house to replace her.

When she arrived and walked in the back door, Karina and Jan were in the kitchen. Karina was stuffing bed linen into the washing machine and looked up in amazement.

"Wow! You never said you would be coming back home?" Karina said. Jan was too surprised to say anything.

Karina starts a Backpackers Business.

Her emotions at seeing Jan in the kitchen were incredible as if she had been missing him. She hugged him and offered to make coffee.

Karina told them both that she would be moving out. She was offered an opportunity to run a backpacker's business while living there.

"That is amazing. So you are in charge, you like that." Her feelings were as if she was another person. Unbelievable. Why would she ever think of leaving Jan?

When Karina left for her room, she joined Jan in the lounge

"Jan, I want to give our marriage another go." I realized that I had been wrong in neglecting you in many ways. Hearing herself saying it was as if another her was speaking. She meant every word she said, and later, in the bedroom, they made love as if it was for the first time.

The following morning, Jan spoke on the phone with someone he seemed to know very well. When she asked who he was talking to, he said it was a girlfriend who he had to break up with

"How long have you known her," she asked while making breakfast.

"For about seven years, she has worked at the terminal office. Her husband is still living with her. He has a serious heart condition, and she still has two teenagers at home. She is the only breadwinner."

Jan had never said so much in one sentence.

"I told her you have returned for good and are my first love."

Jan had planned to drive up to Johannesburg to see his sister in three days, so she was looking forward to the trip.

Visiting Jan's. Sister in Johannesburg

Driving together and passing Bloemfontein brought back memories of Lucas's time in the SA army. After the city, they stopped at a petrol station to fill up and have lunch. She still felt content and happy but wondered how it was possible. She had asked for proof, and she got it. How was it possible that her feelings of being in love were real?

The days they spent time with Hilly were somewhat tiresome. Hilly was a reborn Christian and repeatedly made sure that they knew it. Jan never reacted and tried to stay silent or change the subject.

On the way home, she dropped into a deep depression. The happy feelings of being in love were gone. The sense of being in love was no longer there. How would she ever be able to pick up the pieces in this relationship and make it work? What formula was there for her to use to earn her freedom?

Jan noticed that she had changed and did not know what to say or how to reply. Instead, she suggested a new idea of starting a bed and breakfast business. Justine had suggested that a while ago, since they lived around the corner from the airport and had three bedrooms, She would not look for a job.

She needed to earn money to pay off the credit card debt she accrued during her 6-week trip, and she wanted to finish her novel and pay for the Durban editor.

Starting a B&B with Two rooms Downstairs

"Jan, you have to be quiet when you walk to the kitchen in the morning she whispered. " She warned him before he left the bedroom. His morning farts almost seemed intentional.

They had regular one-night guests and bus drivers who needed to stay overnight and left early, around 6 in the morning. She would have their breakfast box ready. They were easy guests.

Some were not so pleasant, but it was easy money.

She started to give afternoon drawing classes again, but this time, she called them Art analogue doodle therapy classes – drawing through the higher self. For those classes, she again did a lot of photocopying at Jan's office after working hours.

She was far more stable emotionally, and Jan was trying with remarks to push her buttons, but it started to go over her head. Sometimes, she even agreed and laughed at him. She knew that she was initially freeing herself from him emotionally. Soon, it would have to be physical, but she had to take it slowly. There was little mental connection, which was sometimes hard to live with, but her friends, books, and the internet articles made up for it.

Often, the synchronicity she experienced made her aware that an entity from higher realms was overseeing her, but she could not prove that. So, she kept it primarily to herself. She shared it with Ingrid, who suggested seeing the psychic Ingrid had often heard about. So she made a booking and was wondering what that would be like. She was never drawn to other people who wanted to tell her future, but Ingrid said she would never do that.

When she entered the ordinary psychic hallway, another woman greeted her and ushered her into a waiting room with a curtain leading to another room. After what might have been ten minutes, the psychic entered, asking her to follow her into her office. Her appearance was nothing that she expected. She would have thought she was somebody's grandmother if she had met her elsewhere. Very ordinary.

"I usually ask for guidance and meditate on what service I can give to a client, so all I want to know from you is, what would you like to know?"

"She had already had an answer ready." She had not told her anything about her.

"I would like to know if I would ever find my soul purpose."

The woman closed her eyes, indicating she did not want to say anything. She waited to wonder what she would get for an answer.

"I see a man in your life; he is important to you, and together, you stay looking over a kind of railing into the water below."

All she could think was her dad on the ship or even Jan when she was sailing with him. The woman shook her head as if to say, no, that is not it.

"I see no end? That is unusual. You will live a very long life with no end. That is all. "

Well, she was out before she knew it. She did leave some notes in a bowl but was never asked for money. No ending, meaning she would not die? It made her think of a website she had found months ago.

Chapter Twenty-One

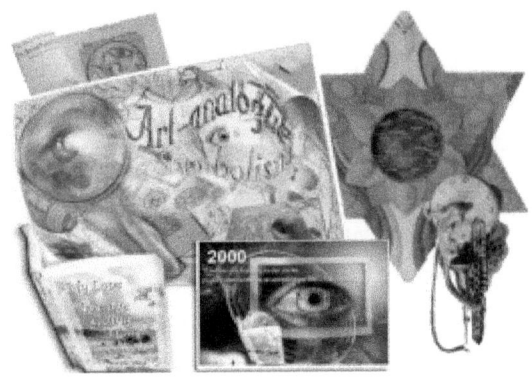

The School for Ascension Website

She had seen this website when she had been scrolling the net. What she read was so interesting, she had become a member. The writings gripped her so much that her time on the internet became an almost daily addiction, especially to see if there was a reply to the emails she kept sending to the organizer.

They were writing about what ascension meant: shifting or transforming our physical body into a light or immortal body. She had learned a great deal about the seven-body vortices and the kundalini and about having a Light body, Or more an etheric body, or like a non-physical copy body she had included into the story of her character Tulanda. Still, she already knew that her first novel would be more about how to manifest anything into this reality.

217

Their daily lives were the same as before her overseas trip, except for her bed and breakfast business, which she only did for the money. It came easy, and her credit card was paid off.

As always, they read the newspapers, but she was not looking for a job until a large university advert caught her eye.

It was all about a university course to become a marriage counsellor. Something pressed her to investigate as if someone was looking over her shoulder.

She was already apprehensive at the idea, knowing about her dyslexic obstacle and her nursing diploma from Holland. They were all burned in the fire. She filled in an application with Jan's help. He was surprised but not impressed about the fee that it would cost.

"You are not paying for it, so why mention any cost?"

Signing up as a Student at University

At her first interview with three teachers to see if she qualified for the course, she told them verbally about her background, including her nursing in Holland and that she had been a lifeline counsellor for several years.

They asked several questions, and after they debated with each other, they returned to her saying. It's not for us necessary to see diplomas due to your age—and life experiences. Congratulations, I hope you will finish the course. He explained that the university course was subsidized with the understanding that she would become a volunteer counsellor for a year. After that, she could start earning a salary.

She did not share this with Jan, who would immediately complain.

She was one of the oldest in the class at forty-seven. The lecturer asked her how long she had been married. She had to think.

"Twenty-seven years, she replied."

None of the students were married, but they were in relationships, and some had psychology degrees.

"Then we have a very experienced student in our class."

Months went by, and her novel had to be re-edited. She enjoyed the process and learned a lot from it. Her English improved, and the spell checker was a great help and will always be. Her romantic interwoven story between two people, Toon and Ingrid, made her feel as if it was her vision board.

Sometimes, she would walk into the supermarket pretending to be her character, Ingrid, who would meet Toon. The feeling that went with it made it all the more enjoyable. It always lifted her spirit when her present reality sometimes got her down. Her storytelling became like a vision board.

Jan wanted to book a flight to Holland to visit his parents. She would be pleased to go along if he paid for it, and she asked if it was okay if she would meet up with some people she met on the Internet who would be in the UK when they visited Sonja.

At first, Jan was sour about that, but since it was only four days, he consented. He would have Sonja on his own.

Visiting Holland with Jan

None of the family knew about their troubled marriage, and Jan did not want them to know about his affairs. He had several after the woman he was with the longest died suddenly from a heart attack. She never confronted him, but she knew. She learned a great deal from her university course all about sexual addictions in men and women that often were the cause of divorce. Jan fitted that bill very well.

Her First Ascension Workshop in the UK

Sonja knew about her four days away and was okay about it. Her flat was terrific, and she had taken free time off work as a flight attendant to be with them.

She travelled by train to the ascension conclave, which they called it, which was held in a luxurious hotel. It reminded her of Diana's venue in Colorado Springs.

She shared a room this time with one woman who travelled from Canada. She had many health issues to do with food. It was her first time learning about gluten intolerance.

There was one man from South Africa in the group called Garry. As she wanted to be called, the facilitator, Mila, was a big, heavy-set gipsy looking, overpowering woman. Her outfits were long, colourful, caftan-like dresses to hide her bulk. Each participant had a private interview with her and Thomas Weber "Oa", her partner, who is equally oversized and overweight.

Mila went into a trance-like state to read her energy levels. They were to her satisfaction so that she could join the intensive workshop. That was a surprise to her since she had already paid upfront.

Later, she heard that two people were told to go home. The experience of seeing entities speaking through Karen Danrich called Mila was impressive. At one stage, Mila was angry at an entity that had, according to her, jumped into a girl from Germany. She screamed and threw an energy ball into the electrical box in the corner, and to everyone's surprise, they were all plunged into darkness. So was the rest of the Hotel!

Inwardly, she was not always sure if she liked the way Mila was more or less preaching, but it did fascinate her.

Their return to Port Elizabeth went very peacefully, but she now knew she needed her bedroom by herself.

Working for Famsa

Apart from being a qualified marriage counsellor, she must finalize her separation. Moving into a separate bedroom upstairs and learning to live in the same house as friends was difficult. Jan found that difficult, unable to see the difference, except that they no longer sleep together.

They followed the same routine, and this time, they shared in the cooking. She was a vegetarian, and he had to accept that.

They did not fight as much anymore. Now and then, Jan tried commenting on her New Age interests in a derogatory way, but she did not respond like she used to. She did not need his approval anymore.

Being emotionally free from Jan did not mean She had no love for him; it was just different. The freedom to do her own thing but living in the same house as the father of her children was a unique experience. However, it was more difficult for Jan. He drank more glasses of wine in the evenings before dinner.

"Hey, you, do not develop alcoholism!" Talking to a man who slurs his words is not pleasant.

"I'm not, but life is not fun anymore."

"Then go out, meet other people, women if you will."

"So you do not have any physical needs anymore?" He slurs. She would not admit that she did not, but was no longer attracted to Jan in that way. She questioned if she ever was. She held back her words. She did not need to hurt him.

"I'm so busy with art therapy classes, counselling at Famsa and finalizing my novel. So gradually, we no longer have to have B& B quests."

Jan was coming home late, so she left his dinner in the oven if it was her day to cook. Sometimes, she was upstairs in her bedroom when she heard him coming home.

She suggested selling the house and going their separate ways, but Jan was not ready. He now wanted to go for counselling.

"If you had suggested that years ago, my reaction would have been different, but not now. Jan, I do not want to grow old with you. Instead, I want to stay friends."

"If only you gave our marriage the same attention as you do to your other activities, then we would not be in this situation. "They were sitting outside on the patio having a glass of wine after having learned that Sonja would be coming to a visit. Now that she is an air hostess, she flies at a very low rate.

"True, I have been having an affair with Spirit while you slept around during our last almost thirty years, but I do not want to split up as enemies. I want to stay friends. Can you do that?"

At Famsa, she had been dealing with couples who needed to learn how to go their separate ways when the relationship had nothing to offer. She gave the clients who had reached that stage ideas taken from their sharing, which each found important or liked.

Sonja Came for a Visit on her Own

"It's so nice to have you home for a week. It will not be long, but I hope you are okay with driving to St. Frances Bay with Dad. Over the weekend, I want to rent a furnished holiday home for a year and to do that, I need half the money from the house sale, but your dad is unwilling to help."

It was refreshing to have Sonja at home without her older partner. They did not hear much from Lucas; apart from that, his baby boy was now four months old, and he had sent photos. Sonja was still living with Frank, and they had to accept their relationship so long as they never married, but she kept quiet about that. She hoped that that relationship would break up in due course.

When she was at Famsa, Sonja had spent time with Jan, so hopefully, he now saw that their home belonged to them both. After all, her inheritance paid off the bank loan.

St. Frances Bay with Jan and Sonja

She made a picnic basket with coffee on the way to St. Frances Bay, hoping an outing would help Jan change his mind about selling the house.

The house that the agent showed her was perfect. It belongs to a family in Johannesburg who only wanted to move in over December month.

"So if you do not mind moving out during December, you can have it."

Putting the House Up for Sale

As an estate agent, her friend Justine found a property for Jan to buy with half the house's money if it was sold for the right price.

Showing Jan the house just one street away was a stroke of luck; he liked it and saw the potential to split the home into two, making a rental unit. He agreed to put the home on the market, and they stipulated the price so Jan could put an offer in with half the money from the house.

The value of the double-story house was an easy sell, and the neighbour on the corner was keen to buy it as an extension to his B and B business. Doors were opening. Jan made an offer on the other property, and they accepted it.

House is Sold

During the weeks that it would take for the transfer, she knew that a new car was better for her than sitting with the old B M W as a woman on her own, but selling her old car was only possible if she had enough money on her bank account, so in the meantime, her Famsa counselling bookings were was still ongoing and so were her art-therapy classes.

Her literary agent was happy with the novel, so she had to learn to write a synopsis of the manuscript and send a printed copy to several New Age publishers worldwide.

Finding a Publisher for her First Novel

Several copies of her manuscript were sent out, and within a few weeks, she received three rejections via email. There was no explanation why, so the disappointment did affect her, but her literary agent had warned her.

She invested more money to send a few more copies of her manuscript and let it go. Too many other things needed her attention.

Selling any leftover leather goods was number one on her to-do list. Then, the leather skins and materials, plus her leather carving tools. That wasn't easy initially since so many memories were attached to them.

"Hendrika, why don't you put your leather till for auction?" Justine had popped in for a glass of wine.

"You think it might sell?"

"Who knows, but it is only an old crappy glorified till that will only open a draw, and it weighs a ton"?

"I feel it will; what have you got to lose?"

"Oh, and who will carry it to the venue where the auction is held?" they both looked at Jan, saying nothing. He was smoking his pipe and started with his second glass of wine, offering Justine a top-up. She had enough. One glass was all she could drink. She would rather have had a Gin and Tonic, but no Martini was in the house.

"I see that I cannot get out of that." She hugged him as if to say thanks.

She knew Jan was deep-down unhappy, but that would happen. He had been going out with another woman from a hiking club he became a member of, and she hoped he found the right partner for his sake and hers.

She was amazed at how okay she was to go through all the changes, but she had an inner knowing that her life would steer in the right direction.

Dividing Household Goods

"Jan, I must pack and sell off my leather tools and stock. Can you not pack anything you want to keep?"

"No, I will leave it all to you. You started it all. "

She started packing the house when it was sold. Splitting most of the kitchen stuff in half. Jan would take all the furniture. And electrical appliances. She was moving into a furnished home, and where she would land afterwards was still a wait-and-see. Having to sit with a lot of household goods was not an option.

The Auction Date Arrived.

Jan somewhat unwillingly took the old leather-covered till to where the auction was held. She had never been to one, so that was a new experience.

"I tell you now, it will never be sold."

"Pssst, why are you being so negative?"The three of them followed the auctioneer, and when the till was brought forward on a trolley, the bidding started. Three people seem to be interested.

"Well, well, they are bidding on it?"

"R500 - R800 – R1000.-.R1500.-. "she now grabbed Justine and Jan from pure excitement. It fetched R3000.

"So, what are you saying now!" Jan kept shaking his head, being so surprised he found it hard to believe.

Buying her First New Car

A few weeks later, her BMW was sold, and she had purchased her new metallic blue Ford Fiesta out of the box from her part of the money.

Jan had organised an open removal truck for himself and suggested she could use it after he moved around the corner.

Her boxes were already organised. Jan never did any packing; he left it all to her, so she divided all the kitchen, linen and even her leather wall art. He was interested in having them on his wall in his new place. Jan also wanted some of her parent's photos. She wondered if he wanted to hang on to our past.

Jan would keep Sonja's cat, Picasso, while Joris came with her.

"Are you still not interested in moving into my flatlet?" Jan kept drinking glasses of wine. I knew he was distressed, but for how long had I not prepared him for their total breakup? Had he truly never believed she would do it?

"You know my reply, Jan. We have been together for far too long. Our interests and viewpoints of life are so different; let's stay friends."

The open transport took three trips alone for all his plants from the greenhouse. And one trip for most of the furniture and boxes I had packed for him. She made sure her boxes were separated, and the driver must have picked them laboriously off the street because she had to keep an eye on her stuff.

She had already packed her new metallic blue Fort Vista car with leather art, computers, clothing and personal stuff like photo albums. There was just enough space for Joris to sleep in his doggy basket on top of things in the passage seat. She'd given him a sleeping pill from the vet so he would doze during the two-hour drive.

When she followed the truck out of Port Elizabeth, to her horror, she saw at least two boxes flying off the back into the road. No matter how hard she hooted, the driver just raced along, being in a hurry.

Three black labourers jumped off with two of her boxes when she drove past the Walmer location. She was fuming, but what could she do? This blatant theft left her in such a state she needed to calm down.

Thank goodness she had packed most of the most valuable items in her car, but there was no room for the leather jackets, skirts and belts she would sell at markets from her new place. And all her paintings and paintings?

Joris slept all the way.

Chapter Twenty-Two

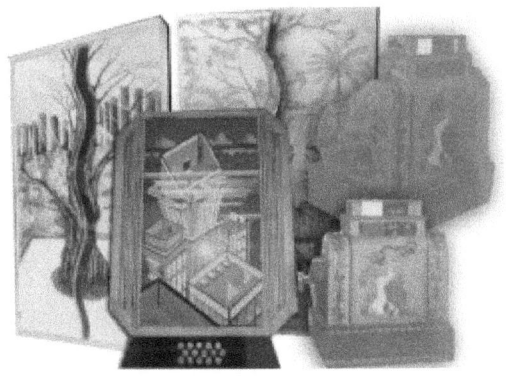

Living Isolated in St Frances Bay

The next day, she woke up from the silence. Joris was awake, looking at her and wanting to jump onto the king-size bed.

"Let's go downstairs and explore the neighbourhood before I unpack."

"Joris was excited, running back and forward, walking to the beach, which was not far away. As a holiday town, most houses were unoccupied. There was hardly anyone on the beach except for a couple with a long-haired dog. Joris wanted to play, but that was not received very well. The tall man grabbed his dog by the collar and told him not to be so unfriendly, all in Dutch.

His wife Maria took to her straight away and invited her for coffee.

The isolation was somewhat challenging initially, but it was great for writing. Hendrika had set up her computer with a dial-up phone link to receive emails.

A Family Visit.

Jan visited with his sister, trying to make her return, but she was not emotionally involved anymore and wished him the best.

His sister did not say much; they must have talked about her New Age and cult attractions, Jan called it, but it did not bother her anymore. She was, for the first time, honouring herself.

Justine and Karina were also regular visitors, and there was enough room to sleep over, having three bedrooms. She created a CV, posted it online with some employment agencies, and let it go into the universe.

Paying for her living expenses from the capital in her bank account was tricky. She needed to earn an income. With the help of Maria, her new Dutch friend who knew many people in St Frances Bay, her first art-analogue workshop was a great success.

Garry, the man from PE she met in the UK during the ascension workshop, also visited one day and suggested she send her manuscript to a South African published in Cape Town called Kima Global Publishers. She has sent so many manuscripts by mail; from now on, she has done it via email. That was a lot cheaper, but I still had no luck.

"I think I approached that publisher via email when I explained my whole ascension series project. That would eventually consist of five different novels, thinking he might be interested. I did get a reply. They were not into fiction and could not take on five books."

They were having an afternoon snack on her back Terrace. The weather was still very mild for the time of the year.

"Try again. You might have scared them off, and they might have forgotten about you anyway."

"Yes, I will; what have I got to lose? This time, I will now use my writer's name.

A Publisher for my First Novel.

The literary agent was not in favour of approaching a local publisher because they would not have a global reach, but since she had not found any, she sent an email with the synopses to Kima Global. She had a look online to see if they had a website. There was one, and she saw a few books on her topic. She even knew one author, Simon Peter Fuller, who had been a speaker at the ACT Centre.

In the meantime, her second character, Richard de Jong, had primarily been on her mind, and she decided to start writing a sequel to her first novel, My Love We Are Going Home.

The emails from the spiritual school of Ascension kept her updated, and another intensive meeting would be this time in Norway.

Settling into living on her own was, at first, not as easy as she hoped. She was now alone and sometimes did not see another person for weeks. Maria and her husband were the only people she could visit; most of the others from her art classes were just students and nothing more.

Maria was very ill. She had already been for chemotherapy treatment and had her breasts removed in Holland, but her cancer had returned. They became close in the short time she got to know her. Maria was dying.

She received an email from the Cape Town publisher with a name like Robin, but the synopses were unclear, so she asked to send the manuscript. They were interested. It would be their first visionary fiction novel.

The publisher did explain why she needed an advanced payment of an amount that she could recuperate as a new author by selling a hundred novels she would buy from them at a wholesale price. It seemed very fair since she was very unknown.

She was so in the clouds that for the whole day, all she could do was walk on the beach with Joris. She had done it!

The First Birthday of her Grandson

She had set her mind on seeing how Lucas was doing in New Zealand, and now that she could travel on stand-by free tickets from London, she had talked it over with Sonja. Getting to London was at her cost, but she would fly to Washington from then on while Sonja was the stewardess on the same flight. Sonja earned double if flying on birthdays. Sonja would turn thirty. Her present would be a laptop she purchased over the internet. It would be delivered to the hotel where they were staying. It was all planned before she arrived in London.

Seeing Sonja in uniform made her proud. She served first-class passengers while her mother had a seat in business class.

Washington

When they arrived in Washington, Sonja had booked a double room because of her and her mom's birthday. The hotel manager had given them a room with a jacuzzi.

A parcel had been delivered and put on the bed. Hendrika hoped it was the laptop.

"Wow, who would have known about my birthday unless it was Frank?"

When Sonja opened it and read the card, she knew it was from her mother.

"Wow, how did you manage all that?"

"Through the internet on a dial-up connection," she laughed.

Sonja spent her free day in Washington walking around the city in summer temperatures.

"I found a publisher for my novel."

"Oh, Mom, congratulations!"

On the flight back to London, Sonja booked her into a flight to New York with a connecting flight to Los Angeles, all on a stand-by ticket.

"Give Lucas my love, Mom. I hope he is happy. Tell him I will visit him soon. "

Her seat was in first class to New York. It was a night flight, so she had an almost single-bed chair. What a luxury.

Los Angeles

Arriving in Los Angeles was almost terrifying. They were renovating the roof structure at the terminal, where she had to wait for a standby ticket to become available to Auckland, which could take hours. She waited for almost six hours while masses of people streamed past her.

There were no seats for her to sit near the boarding desk, so she had to listen carefully when her name would be called, so she had to perch on her suitcase.

Suddenly, all she saw, instead of people, was their human bodies changing into streaming colours, all moving united into a kind of symphony. The moment her mind questioned what she saw, in an instant, the colours became people again.

In a daze, she vaguely heard someone calling her name. She had a seat on the plane to Auckland in the business class.

Auckland

Her arrival in Auckland was full of happiness at the prospect of seeing Lucas again, waiting for her at arrival, but there was nobody. She waited and waited and found a call box to call. That wasn't easy at first, not having local coins. She was now apprehensive.

"Moms! I'm so sorry I lost track of time. I will come and fetch you!" her image of seeing him at the airport greeting her clattered into a heap from the disappointment.

It took an hour for Lucas to arrive. By this time, she was exhausted. He explained that Melany, the mother of his child, was furious that she was coming. She was unprepared to see his mother, so they had a major row.

She took it all in and knew that her stay was over eighteen days, of which she would spend half of it with Karina's mom on the tip of the north island.

Her arrival at a wooden-looking freestanding home with kids' toys on the front lawn and a heavyset woman in a dressing gown was an emotional shock, but she would not show that. Instead, she greeted her as if a mother-in-law were hugging her. She would be as pleasant and grateful to her as she could. It was a mess inside, but Melany had made a place for her to rest in her sewing corner off the lounge.

All she wanted was to sleep. Her body had been through such a rollercoaster; she apologised to them both after picking up a one-year-old cute little boy with big eyes like his dad.

Lucas went to work, so she made the best of a difficult situation on the first day. Her grandchild was a joy to observe, making all the difference. She was allowed to bathe him while his mother got dressed.

Mel showed her the piecework she had done for a factory, sewing collars for men's shirts. There was a bag for her to work on.

"Let me do it, and I'm good at sewing. You do what you need to do. It will give me the feeling of being useful." That was not what Lucas' girlfriend expected, but another child of around eight was timid and getting ready for school.

Their days together were working out fine. Lucas drove them all to Melany's mother, who lived in Taupo, an hour away. She was welcomed by the other grandmother, who said, "I will allow you to spend time with your grandson, but he is ours." She never showed the inner turmoil she felt about these people. The fact that they loved Lucas and were very proud of him made up for it.

She was shown around as a tourist first to Rotorua, walking on a narrow path between bubbling mud pools, shooting geysers, and looking at what volcanic scenery would look like. The other grandmother took her to a natural hot spring, and Lucas drove up to Mount Taranaki with the two kids in the snow.

The stepdad owned a sailing boat he took out regularly, and he invited her to join when they competed in a sailing race on the largest lake in the central North Island. Lucas was a deckhand and learned a lot of sailing rules while she tried getting out of their way. She was freezing in the open water of the lake.

The time had arrived to travel by bus to the top of the north island, where Karina's mom was waiting at the bus stop. What a lovely woman. She made her feel very welcome. She hoped to find them all in a better space when she drove back to Hamilton after a few days.

She joined them on the couch, cheering the SA All Blacks rugby team on the TV and took them all shopping the day before she left to fly back to London via New York with a connecting flight to Johannesburg and PE.

Lucas' new family took her to the airport, saying goodbye to her as a loved mother and grandmother.

Joining an Ascension Workshop in Norway.

Once a month, she would drive to PE and stay for the day with Justine and her Dad, doing her grocery shopping for a month and other errands. Her capital at the bank was shrinking after her trip to Lucas because she spoiled them on her credit card as if she were a millionaire. The journey to Norway to the SSOA workshop was scary financially, but she needed to go. Joris would be staying with Justine.

Norway was beautiful but very cold, and it was mid-winter, and the hotel was very posh. The food was included in the cost of the workshop. She had never seen so many dishes all made with fish.

More information on the Language of Light started to inspire her since the energy so related to her Art Analogue doodling classes. She told Mila about it and said she could give classes during her next intensive in Canada. Mila said she would publish many books, but it should be with the Spiritual School Of Ascension. She did not have the heart to say she had already found a publisher.

She had regular emails from her publisher, and it felt like she was writing to a woman friend. Her insight into her book was amazing. She was very kind, and they shared personal ideas about life. She knew nothing about the personal life of her publisher.

Back Home in St Frances Bay

The moment she was home, that was what she would do: prepare for her workshop in Canada. Maybe that is where her future income would come from. Together with her first novel, she was confident that she was on the right path.

The Ascension Workshop in Canada

Her art therapy classes in St. Frances Bay prepared her for the Language of Light workshops in Canada. Her students would draw out the qualities for themselves.

There were five people in her new doodling class, including Maria. In her introduction, she had already explained what her workshop was all about.

"Imagine that your blueprint codes are on a large screen. They are telling you that the energy is right for you to take your power back." She said in a soft voice while music was playing. Many coloured pens in the centre were for everyone to use on their large sheet of paper.

Everybody was doodling their symbols that would stand for a soul quality they needed to embody during this lifetime. Soon, she will be doing this workshop in Canada.

"Transform the energy of the virtues you have embodied into your etheric body through your chakra portals to become the language of your soul. Become again the soul who drew up the original blueprint, the plan that would serve you now. "Your soul's journey will be awakening in the most grace-filled way."

The colourful scarves she had decorated her classroom with would help bring her students into a meditative mode. She had learned a great deal about how to create an atmosphere from Diana in Colorado Springs.

She had dreamed of seeing herself in a video doing the same thing last night. She was sure that it must have been from her class in Canada.

She had written up what she would say in softly spoken words.

"Your symbols whisper that the time is now for you to re-design your life. You can erase the falsehoods, set aside the pain, forgive yourself for getting off track, forgive those who taught you falsely."

The music she had chosen would, at this moment, be the bumblebee tune.

"You have the power to re-design your path, to get it back on track. To rebuild the foundation of who you are spiritually, your I Am. To become more grounded in your Truth."

She had been reading books written by Rudolf Stainer that she must have read before, but they were making a lot more sense this time around,

The doodling activities had worked for her, so she hoped it would work for those who crossed her path.

"This is the opportunity of the energy that is upon us now. I hope each of you 'hears' or feels the energy of your symbols and transforms your life into the experience of Joy it was always meant to be."

It was her last workshop before leaving to fly to England. She would fly to the United States and Canada on standby tickets for Free! Being Sonja's mother, her job had its perks.

St Frances Bay

Robin, her publisher, wrote to her about the typesetting of her novel and said that the graphic designer could use the cover image she had emailed to her.

While on a dial-up connection to the internet, nobody could call her. She would not hear it ringing. She had purchased her first cell phone in PE, and only Jan, Justine and Karina had her number, so when the landline rang, she was surprised.

"Hello, who is speaking?"

"Me, your publisher." But...it was a male voice that spoke? She was so surprised that she had been corresponding with a guy. Was Robin a man? She was silent for a few moments while her heart was beating.

"I would like to bring your first proof and meet you simultaneously. " His warm, deep voice sounded so familiar. Had she met him before? Wow, Robin wanted to drive from Cape Town to St Frances Bay! She told him that she lived in a three-bedroom cottage and he could stay over since it was a long trip. He was very grateful for her offer.

Robin would contact her again after returning to Calgary, Canada.

For the rest of the day, she could not do anything. Her heart was still fluttering as if he was somebody exceptional.

On the way to PE, dropping Joris at Justine's place, she was still in a fantasy reality, thinking of the publisher she had never met. She looked on the internet, and there was one photo, but it was a man with pure white hair. It was difficult to tell what his age was. All she knew was that she loved his voice.

Port Elizabeth

She dropped off Joris, who would stay with Justine, and before she drove her to the airport, they visited Ingrid and her husband. She told her about her publisher, whom she had been writing to as an online girlfriend, only to find out he was a man!

They all thought that was hilarious.

"Is he married? " Ingrid asked.

"I have no idea; I know nothing about him except that it is as if I heard his voice before."

Flying to London for a second time in a short while was exciting. Sonja would meet her at the airport, showing her where to board for Dallas and from there, she would go to the ticket terminal for Calgary. She was getting the hang of it flying on a stand-by ticket.

Her First workshop in Canada

She carried a lot of papers in her hand luggage to do with the Language of Light workshop she would give because her suitcase was full of warm winter clothes. She read that Calgary was still cold in May.

She was horrified that her connecting flight to Calgary was canceled. She had to sit in the terminal for hours, hoping to get onto the next flight as a standby passenger. She would not be on time for her interview with Mila and OA before the workshop started. She was a nervous wreck when she boarded the next flight.

The taxi took her to the already booked and paid for hotel, including the intensive workshop. Mila told her in an email that she would be paid back for the doodling seminar, which would be handy for pocket money.

She would share it with another participant, who would probably be at the other hotel but not where the conclave intensive was being held. Her suitcase was still unpacked, but she needed to change her clothes. Then they told her where to walk to get to the other hotel. It was not far away.

She could not have warned them why she was being delayed, so she was asked to wait in a reception room. She brought Mila and her partner a bottle of South African wine. She waited for well over an hour before Mila arrived, knowing that the first day of the workshop had already started.

Mile came straight to the point. She was thrown out of the school of ascension due to the drop in her energy that was reflected in her missing her flight.

The hurt and shocked feeling in her solar plexus gave her a stomach cramp

"The flight was cancelled; I never missed it," she replied, half crying.

"Walking the ascension path is very difficult, and it is revealed in your manifestation for being too late that you would not make it. "

"But...what about the workshop I've been preparing for?"

Mila shook her head and told her the woman she shared the room with had to move out if she wanted to stay in the group. Mila got up to return to her workshop and said she could no longer contact anyone.

She left the bottle of wine with their name on it and left. She walked back to her hotel. It was the saddest walk she had ever taken. She had to pay for the double room because the woman she shared with wanted her money back.

She was not going to explain what happened. Instead, she paid for two nights and would have to stay somewhere else in cheaper accommodation before she could fly back to Dallas a week later. She cried for hours and fell asleep. The following morning, she called her publisher because he could only understand her feelings.

Robin was sorrowful for her and angry that she had been thrown out. He told her about a friend who lived in Calgary.

"I will call her because you need a friend in a strange country. "

She received a call from Robin's friend, and they talked for a long time. She did feel better and followed her suggestion to take a bus ride away from Calgary to the town called Banff within Banff National Park.

"My dear, take a break and make the best of a problematic situation by spending four days in the most picturesque provinces in

Canada; you will find some cheaper accommodation before you fly back to London via Dallas. "

She got a brochure about Banff, found a backpacker place where she booked a room for four nights and booked a trip by bus to a large glacier near Victoria Hotel, which was partly closed. She would have to walk around the town the rest of the time.

She was glad for leather boots because the snow was still lying everywhere in May. The town itself reminded her of their tourist town of Knysna. Here, it had an Indian Trading Post with lots of dream catchers.

She saw signs of hot springs and decided to visit those the next day. Gradually, her energy came back. It was not the same as before she left for her trip, but emotionally, she was recovering.

At the hot springs, she met two women younger than she was. Having held her fiftieth birthday months before she left for St Frances Bay, she felt old. They saw that she had spent too long in the hot pools and gave her some sugared drink to recover, feeling faint. They drove into Banff and paid for dinner while she almost became a marriage counsellor. They were going through difficult times.

Her bus ride back to Calgary took one hour, and she went directly to the airport. She would catch a direct connecting flight via Dallas to London with a stopover. Sonja knew she had returned two weeks earlier and would meet her at the airport. She could stay with them at one of Frank's huge homes until she could fly to Holland to spend time with Annemarie.

Her stay was not easy; Sonja was unhappy, and Frank was downright rude after leaving her in the cold in her dressing gown outside while he took Sonja away in his helicopter. The back door had slammed closed, so she could not get back into the house. She walked to the nearest neighbour, who drove her back, climbed into the open-top window, and opened the back door from inside.

When the helicopter returned an hour later, they were surprised that she was inside, so they knew she had been left outside!

"Sonja, can you take me to the airport? I have booked a flight to Amsterdam, but do I have to pay for a taxi?"

She was already packed to leave. She was no longer staying with them. Sonja drove her to the airport crying.

"It's your life, Moppie, but this man is not suitable for you. The way he treated me, while I never said anything to warrant his behaviour and left me outside in the cold, I needed to go. "

"Frank is very stressed; he is going through some challenging times financially."

She never replied but hugged her and walked inside, leaving her to drive back home.

Amsterdam

Annemarie was waiting for her at the airport. Did she look stressed out and thin? Had she lost weight? she asked herself during the drive to Annemarie's home.

She told her why she had to make up for the date so she could fly back to South Africa, and her family were very kind to her. I do not think they truly understood what had happened, and she also had to reflect on why she had to go through this almost spiritual rejection.

Her Return Back to St Frances Bay

Her flight back was full of obstacles. They stopped in Entebbe, Uganda, and all had to get out of the plane due to a bomb scare. Everybody was asked to claim their luggage on the tarmac. The temperature must have been near forty degrees C

She missed her connecting flight to Port Elizabeth, but thankfully, they booked her into the holiday inn, at the cost of the airline, so that she could catch the next flight in the morning.

When she arrived in PE, she must have looked worn out. Karina was shocked. Jan had asked if she could fetch her; he had a ship to attend to, and Justine had a client to show two properties. She was grateful for that. At least she would not explain herself.

Joris greeted her in an abundant way that only dogs do. Justine came home, and the four asked many questions; she only wanted to drive back to St Frances Bay in the car she had left in Justine's driveway.

"I will tell you what happened in due time, but not now. As you all can see, I'm too tired and worn out."

Robin is Coming to Visit

It was August, the weather was still very lovely, and she recovered from her travel ordeals. Her excitement to meet Robin had been on her mind for a week. The entire morning was spent tidying up the place, and as she looked at herself, she still had curlers in her hair when the front door rang.

She was shocked to see Robin, the man from the photo, standing at the other side of the door through the peephole. Joris was barking but had to pull her curlers out of her hair as fast as possible in the downstairs bedroom.

She opened the front door and greeted him like an old friend with a hug. He had such a lovely, kind face, and he was calm. She loved the moment when she looked into his eyes.

Robin stayed for a few nights because he had arranged to see another prospective author who would drive up from outside PE to meet him.

They had a great time together and talked until the early morning. Their connection was instant. She was very attracted to him but in a very different way. It was more like a soul connection, but they did unite physically. He was divorced and lived in Rondebosch. Robin had started his publishing company in 1992.

When he left the following day, they both wished he could stay longer, but he needed to return to his office in Cape Town.

Jolanda lost Piet in a Freak Accident.

The phone call from who she thought was Piet was from Richy, his son. Piet had electrocuted himself and died immediately. The shock of losing a dear friend so suddenly was overwhelming. Poor Jolanda. How was she coping?

"My mom is not coping, and we wondered if she could spend some time with you?" She booked a ticket and paid for it with her accumulated Air miles.

Jolanda's grief was enormous. Whenever they walked onto the beach, she would scream angrily that Piet had left her. She made her do art therapy, which helped, but Jolanda drowned her sorrow in glasses of wine.

She almost felt guilty for feeling so happy inside meeting Robin, who had asked her to come and live with him in Cape Town after his second visit. They had such a loving connection; she was on cloud nine. He knew she could build up her art therapy workshop classes in Cape Town.

Jolanda left for Johannesburg after three weeks and had four weeks to pack up. Robin came once more before she would drive to Cape Town. He took her plants, artwork, and a bicycle fitted into his Uno.

She had booked a removal van for the rest of her stuff and returned the key to the agent with whom she had become very friendly during her stay.

Saying goodbye to Maria was hard; she knew she would not live for long by then.

Driving to Cape Town felt like a new beginning. Her car was packed to the brim, and Joris sat on top, asleep in his basket. It took eight hours to drive to her new home in Rondebosch, where she drove up the driveway.

Robin greeted her with her first printed novel in his hand. They didn't need to talk; he said it said all,

My Love, We Are Going Home

About the Author

Nadine May is a graphic artist, designer, and visionary fiction writer with six published titles. This book represents a new departure for her, being rather about a character who does her best to achieve a self-supporting life under challenging circumstances. It shows what can be achieved by someone with only basic English language skills and no established support base. Products with her designs may be found on her website and here, and all her graphics on products have a Facebook page.

She is the author of:

Book 1 The Reality Shifters (previously titled: My Love We Are Going Home)

Book 2 Orphanage of Souls – republished as one novel

Book 3 Vanishing Worlds -

Meditations of the Language of Light

The workbook The Language of Light

Seven chakra journals on the Language of Light

About the Publisher

In 2001, I published my first novel with Kima Global Publishers. Over the years, I published 12 more titles with the same publisher, who eventually became my husband. Sadly, he passed away in 2023. After much consideration and weighing my options, I have published my two-book series, "The *Self*-Employed Housewife," and the five-book visionary fiction series, "Awakening to our Ascension," under the name 'The Power of Words' through Draft2Digital. I plan to include my workbooks and journals at a later stage. For now, they are still only available locally in SA.

Read more at https://nadinemay.company.site/.